The Searching Glance

LINDA CRACKNELL has been a teacher of English in Zanzibar, worked for environmental charity WWF, and was writer-in-residence at Hugh MacDiarmid's last home near Biggar. She now lives in Highland Perthshire. Her short fiction has appeared in magazines and journals, been broadcast on BBC Radio, and was previously collected in *Life Drawing*, published in 2000. She writes drama for BBC Radio 4 and is now writing essays about walks which follow human stories in 'wild' places.

LINDA CRACKNELL

The Searching Glance

SALT

LONDON

PUBLISHED BY SALT PUBLISHING
Fourth Floor, 2 Tavistock Place, Bloomsbury, London WC1H 9RA United Kingdom

© Linda Cracknell, 2008, 2009

First published 2008
This paperback edition 2009

Printed and bound in the United Kingdom by Lightning Source UK Ltd

Typeset in Swift 11 / 14

ISBN 978 1 84471 441 4 hardback
ISBN 978 1 84471 743 9 paperback

1 3 5 7 9 8 6 4 2

For my mother

Contents

The Smell of Growth

YOU CAN WEAR this one, as you've been a good girl, I say to Pauline. I pull the red mini skirt up over her long thin legs, and then we choose the white T-shirt. Her eyes make a wee rattle as they blink open and shut. I comb out her blonde hair. It feels slick and jangles in the sun coming through the French windows. A small yellow leaf is tangled behind her ear and I ask her, what have you been up to?

Mum pulled up my pyjama top this morning and said the spots are away and I'm probably better, but I should stay off school one more day just to make sure. She makes me tomato soup and toast every lunchtime. It's like a different house during the day—quiet without the boys, and the phone rings loudly, and Mum takes her purse and goes to the shops, and sometimes visitors come. Mum spends most of the day up to her elbows in water, her hands pink in her Marigolds. But this morning she put on a dress and rubbed hand cream on after she washed-up.

Yesterday I felt better enough to go down the garden.

1

Me and Pauline filled our teacups at the pond and chatted, but Mum thought I was hiding because the bracken came way up over my head. She said the water's dirty no wonder I'm ill, and it's a bad place and that there's danger. She doesn't like the wild land at the bottom of the garden which she calls I-despair-of-it. It's just the patio she likes, where the sunshine is. I don't know why she thinks it's bad. There's that smell down there that goes up my nose all hot and thick. Geoff-Next-Door says it's Growth. But I don't think Growth is the same as bad. You don't see robbers down there, or the men who drive too fast like the ones Mum shouts at when she's taking us to school.

Geoff-Next-Door helps Mum with the lawn-mower and he lifts bags of coal for her in the winter. She doesn't know what we'd do without him. But I don't like to look at him because one of his eyes darts about like a wee fish while the other one doesn't blink and looks like he's just woken up. Mum says it's a glass eye.

I watched the tadpoles for ages before Mum found me. They've grown wee legs which wriggle as they swim. I tried to catch one in my hand but it slipped through. I was elbow-deep in the cold water and vanished my hands down below the slime at the bottom. Once I pushed an old bone that I found near the compost heap into the slime and I never found it again. But instead rose up a beautiful string of silver beads in the water that I couldn't catch, just like the tadpole.

Look at you covered in mud, she said, when she found me. Can't you just grow up? She pinched her hand on my wrist and pulled me away from the pond. I've told you. Keep away can't you? I wanted to show her how the tadpoles had changed, but her hand cuffed at me and spurted the tears out.

Today I'm staying indoors. I look out the window and when Nina swooshes up in her car, with her hair flying out the back and her waving hand, I see the line on Mum's forehead fade.

Give your wicked auntie a kiss then, Nina says, although she's not my auntie really. You're just like I was at your age. Legs up to your ears. She pushes my hair behind my ear as if she's looking for the top of my leg there. I'm growing my hair out, I tell her, and tip my head back till I can feel it tickle my shoulders just like hers and Pauline's does. When she stands up, her dress rustles and a smell whooshes from it like if you get too near the buddleia bush.

She curls my fingers over a packet of sweeties and then takes Mum out into the sunshine. You need some colour in your cheeks, I hear her say. Nina must have been sitting out a lot already. The flat bit where her blouse is open and the necklace glitters, is almost the colour of the barley sugar. I don't open the sweeties yet, in case Mum says I don't deserve them.

Nina's eyes are white around the blue pupil bit,

whereas Mum's always look pink. It's having the three of us to look after on her own and it's not fair. That's what Geoff-Next-Door says. You be good for her, eh? I nod and it doesn't really feel like a lie but I think he knows that I like to watch tadpoles. I don't mean to catch cobwebs and twigs in my hair, and I'm always sorry when I hear Mum crying in her bedroom. Sometimes I have to pinch the soft white bits under the boys' arms if they do mischief. That's what growing up means—not getting muddy, or leaving things on the sitting room floor. It means wearing Marigolds, and not having toys like children do. We have to learn to be good like Mum or Nina are. Pauline's nearly good too.

When they come in, Mum tinkles keys and Nina's handbag goes snip-snap. Your mummy needs a bikini, darling. Shall we three girls go on a shopping trip, mmm? They've lovely ones at the Outlet store and they're half the price. Her long eyelashes go bat, and out of the big snip-snap bag she pulls her gold lipstick case. There's a wee mirror attached to it, and she pins back her mouth as she paints, cross-eyed in the mirror. She eats her lips together and makes a pout at me, then laughs. She rustles down, pointing the lipstick at my mouth, and says, go like that, and makes that funny face again. I look at Mum. Just this once, she says, and she's almost smiling and her lips have changed colour too.

In the car the wind slaps down my eyes, and I push

Pauline's shut for her. Nina has dark glasses on so she can drive. When we get there, she pulls her scarf off and brushes her hair. I have to comb Pauline's too. I'm almost at the end of my, Mum says, and then she stops speaking and her head drops. And Nina puts a hand on her shoulder and snip-snap out comes the hanky. She swings my hand as we cross the car park. We'll find your ma something bright to cheer her up, eh?

In the Outlet store it's noisy. Behind a screen are rows of sewing machines galloping along material with ladies driving them. There's a cash register by the door, but no one sitting at it like you get in Tesco's. All around the room there's troughs full of plastic bags with different colours showing through them. Pushed underneath the troughs are big cardboard boxes, brimming with more bags the same. On the wall above each trough there's a piece of clothing pinned up to show you what's inside the bags.

Nina tugs Mum about, piling bags in her arms. That's fabby, she says, holding a turquoise one against Mum. Just the thing to set off a tan, and look at it only eleven ninety-nine and it's a genuine Fancini. Nina sends Mum behind the curtain.

There's a pink life-sized doll with long thin legs. She's wearing a bikini with wee gold rings at the side of the knickers and between her boobs, and I say to Pauline, I can just see you in that. We sit under her feet and I pull

Pauline's red skirt straight. We both have tired legs. I suck at my lips but they don't taste like strawberry how they looked in the mirror, not even sweet at all, but like anti-septic or something.

Nina's bag goes snip and makes me look at her. She's leaning over a pool of plastic like she's watching tadpoles swimming between the bags, trying to catch one. I keep quiet because she looks busy in her head, like Mum at the sink with the line across her forehead. That's a pretty one, she says to herself. The snip-snap bag yawns over her arm and the tadpole-catching hand dips below the trough. It's like it belongs to someone else because she's not looking in the cardboard box where it is. The hand looks like a claw with its red nails. It clamps onto a bag of turquoise and scoops it in. Snap, goes the snip-snap bag and Nina moves on to the next trough, paddling again in the pool of plastic.

Mum steps from behind the curtain, undressed except for the orange bikini. Nina puts her hands on her hips like she's looking at a beauty queen. You look fantastic, she flips her head back so her hair slicks like a tail down her back. But Mum has bony bits on her tummy and a label poking out under her arm and you can see her knickers under the bikini bottoms which are very very small. Pauline and I sit at the big doll's feet and blink.

When Mum takes the orange bikini and calls the lady to the cash register, Nina doesn't say anything about the turquoise one that she chose. She doesn't even try it on. And the bag doesn't snip or snap to get out her purse. When we get back into the car, I look at Nina's face, close up, as she turns to speak to Mum. She's eaten off some of her lipstick and underneath she's a purple-pink colour. I see for the first time that she has lines drawn in red on the outside of her nostrils, like wee cracks in a blackbird's egg shell. Over the top of them there's a soft pink dusting, like sherbet.

After lunch, Nina leaves. She kisses Mum and then me. Her lipstick is quite worn away now. She left it on the edge of the glass she was drinking from—a sticky print like a slug's skin, all puckered up, like when you poke them with sticks in the garden. When she gets in the car, she stares into the mirror. And I want to ask her if she's going back to the Outlet because she's forgotten that you have to give money when you buy something.

You've got very quiet says Mum to me. Maybe you're not quite better after all. She's put on her orange bikini but this time without knickers underneath and she stretches on the sunlounger, all pink and shiny. I sit beside her for a while but she has her eyes closed, and when I say Mum, Nina is a good girl isn't she, she just smiles a little at one corner of her mouth and mutters, Girl? Lady, then, I say. And she breathes, Go inside, rest.

I take the Marigolds from the sink and creep past Mum and down the garden with Pauline. Geoff-Next-Door is vrooming his lawnmower, but I don't look at him. His hand goes up in the corner of my eye.

I take off her red miniskirt. And I unpeel the white T-shirt. When she's naked, I put her in the water, wearing the Marigolds to keep my hands dry and soft like Mum's. She floats with one arm up above her head like she's waving goodbye, and a leaf sticks on her tummy. But she doesn't look right because her eyes are still wide open, staring blue into the sky. So I take her out again and push the lashes of one eye down so I just see the pink hood. The other eye is full of water and won't shut. My finger doesn't work properly with the floppy end of the Marigolds, so I pick up a stick. I push the eye shut with it. Then I push it harder. It makes a snapping noise and goes into her head, so far that I can see she's hollow and dark red inside, not pink. When I've done both her eyes I put her back in the pond and with the Marigolds up to my elbows I can push her all the way down to the bottom. Her hair waves like a bright seaweed, fading.

Lastly rises the string of silver beads that I try to catch in my hand. And in amongst the bracken, the smell of Growth oozes in my nose.

Over the Garden Wall

His lips sent beads of the recent rain quivering down the waxy red curve of the frangipani petal. The sun had reclaimed the sky again, crashing black shadows onto the ground and returning colours to primary. But drips still beat onto the lower foliage of the garden, flicking leaves up and down like piano keys with no apparent player. It was the first time that the frangipani bush had flowered, and he lingered over it with his face and fingers and his inhalations, soaking in the sense that it was only there because of him, because he had planted and nurtured it. Now he would be the one to enjoy it.

Someone from home had written to congratulate him on his garden 'retreat'. Outrage advanced on him in the hours after reading the letter. As if he was the sort of man to retreat. He had written back straight away, saying quite to the contrary, he considered his garden an 'attack'. Hadn't his campaign involved taking possession of the land, a blitz on the scrambling native bush, a colonisation of the fragrant and the flamboyant? And wasn't he right now safeguarding his territory, securing its borders?

He had set a flame to the letter with its impertinent P.S. —'So sorry to hear'.

His world was complete. Mangoes fell, ready sliced onto his plate; prawns, by the bucketful. There was always a cold beer to cool his throat as he stared from his bar terrace across the Indian Ocean. The heavy curve of a young shark's backbone over the back of a bicycle would soon be straightened as he carried it to his kitchen. He could drive to another beach if he wanted to, or perhaps to the bar on the west where the sunsets were better.

Everywhere he went, people straightened their backs in the fields or turned mid-purchase in the market, and raised a hand in the air for him. And they called out his name—children and adults. He couldn't hear them because the air-conditioning didn't work properly unless the car windows were shut. But he saw his name in the shape of their lips. It made him rise upright in his seat. Even though they gave it freely, he was determined to deserve their respect—the man who, with the barest soil on this hard white coral rock of an island, had made frangipani and bougainvillaea blossom, and filled the night air with the scent of ylang-ylang.

He relished the world he had created as he drew on his cigar underneath the stars and the moon, listening to the dark crash of the waves. The night air was full of the trilling creatures he had attracted. He didn't know whether the disembodied sounds were made by birds, insects, frogs maybe. And he didn't want to see, in case they were ugly scuttling things that would make him want to pull his bare feet away.

Even during the day much of his time was spent on the terrace with a beer in one hand, gazing out across his own private lagoon, with his garden hooting and trilling behind him. He played in whispers with the similar sound of the words 'lagoon' and 'saloon'. He had both here, two-in-one, he joked to himself. He did that—played with words, plaited and unravelled them. Recently, 'stronghold' and 'stranglehold' had come into his head together—unrelated, and yet so similar in sound. A lifetime of cross-word puzzles must have done that to him. The mind sparring with itself.

About a mile out, he could see waves breaking over the reef—he could hear them, in fact. Boats would come edging through the shallows, working their way a few miles south to the break where an underwater cliff sheered downwards and they could escape, to fish the deeper sea. At first he had felt that the turquoise water of the lagoon belonged to him. He had wanted the boats to stay out. The *dhows* and poled canoes, and rickety dug-outs with their outriggers had the whole of the purple-blue sea beyond the reef as their realm. He wasn't going to take that from them. But as time went on he had noticed that the boats scudding along the lagoon didn't interrupt the stark whiteness of his coral beach by coming ashore. The men's heads turned towards him, and their hands rose. That was all. In the early days he had stood, the captain on his bridge, as they went past. But not now. He just let them pass.

Anyone who looked into his garden could see that life was good because he made it so. After a lifetime of postings and stations here and there, of being exposed to this and that danger, he'd made himself secure. He'd trucked in dark rich soil from the mainland to embed his roots, and imported dried blood and bone meal from Europe. Now he was enclosed by a rising tanglewood of green.

When he drove through the village at night, he saw folk clustered in the lamplight and shadows, and he smelt roasting fish. There was laughter and music from a tinny radio, but no electricity, and he saw that they used the most basic of implements. With his garden, he had shown them what was possible, how they didn't need to live on top of each other in huts full of charcoal smoke, and stand in their doorways each dawn to sweep at the hard coral they had chosen to support their lives.

As the garden's riches had grown, it had drawn in intruders. More sweet almonds must hit the ground than remained under the tree in the morning, and it wasn't just the fruit bats to blame. The rustle and thump behind him at dusk was surely someone raiding the mango tree. Paths with an ancient, bare-foot quality began to appear. The white sandy trails worn amongst the trees reminded him of through-routes across wasteland, between housing estates, in his long lost past. And he didn't want to be reminded of the trickle of sweat down his back. Running through the scrub from the sound of pursuing footsteps. The Barr Boys next door and his mother reminding him, 'We're polite to neighbours, aren't we, now?'

No one wanted thieves in their garden.

There were dogs, too. He heard them at night, roaming and howling as a pack. And he heard the squeals of their victims. The dogs scavenged for waste at the back doors of hotels, collectively wolfish. (How similar 'dog' was to 'god', he noticed. And yet gods were singular. A 'pack of gods' was unthinkable.) He didn't want dogs in his garden, either.

The disappearing fruit and the dogs hadn't galvanised him though, on reflection. It was the trouble that started things. Gangs of young men, fired up with—what? Hunger? He shook his head, doubted it. (He made a mental note at the same time though, of the similar sound of 'hunger' and 'anger'.) Drugs, perhaps. Or just fired up by being young men. They came with *pangas* and slashed at people and property. The Italian hotel owner a few miles down the coast had to be helicoptered out with his injuries. Word was it was an orchestrated attack, outsiders, probably from the mainland.

It was true that the thick, rich foliage he had created around himself provided perfect cover for someone to creep up on him. In the middle of the night, he would sometimes raise his head from the pillow at a sound penetrating the jungle of his dreams. He didn't even open his eyes, and slumped back down to resume sleep as soon as he was reassured. But he began to feel the need for clearer definition where the garden bordered the road to the village—something between the green and the white. And he would get an *askari* too, to act sentry for him at the entrance, an *askari* with a dog.

He dallied with the idea of a thorn hedge—both burglar-proof and beautiful. Like a hostile hedge of holly that he would have thought of to surround the Surrey garden with its roses and striped lawns. The garden he had worked so hard to out-do here. The hedge would be impregnable, ten feet high, five feet in diameter, a strong single species to provide privacy and protection. Our passion for privacy, he thought, that's what makes us different from the people here.

But his plan remained a plan.

The story of the Italian-run hotel reached the British newspapers and she had written saying, 'You told me it was completely safe there—a paradise.' Not long afterwards she wrote again saying how beautiful the azaleas were that spring and how the Fosters had a new spaniel pup, and that she would stay there after all for the summer. And then the final letter saying, 'There's someone else'.

He tripped as he broke through the deep shade of the garden, reading the letter. Sunlight on the terrace flashed off the white page and blinded him for a moment. The jolt fizzed up his heartbeat.

Then he had decided. A hedge would take time to grow. Whereas a wall could materialise quickly.

~

'Mattress?'

'Eheh.'

'Fridge?'

'Eheh.'

'TV?'

'Eheh.'

Hassan met Idi's grunts of assent with incredulity. Was it possible that a boy from his own village would get all these riches? He laughed, slapping his hand against the breeze block wall that Idi sat astride.

'So he pays you in dollars?'

'He will.'

Hassan grew tall. 'I can help you.'

'It's a job for one. That's what he said.'

'You could ask him for me, brother. You know him—

he's your friend.'

'He's my boss. Not my friend.'

'It's the same.'

'I've nearly finished, anyway.'

Idi swung onto the ladder, and climbed down onto the lane that led to the village. He stood back and admired his handiwork—the regular rows of blocks fixed together one on top of the other with cement that set fast in the sun. Many people had come to watch at first. Now the wall stretched on three sides of the man's ground. The fourth side needed no wall; it was delineated by the hard, white slab of the beach, which was regularly patrolled.

'Like New York,' he said to Hassan. 'Wall Street.' And they both laughed, thinking of magazine pictures someone at school had shown them of white men perched high on the towering structure of the Empire State Building. They had presumably got so high by piling block upon block in just the same way.

Hassan lay back in his barrow of coconuts and cracked one open with a blow of his *panga*. He drank and then handed it to Idi. He was taking coconuts to the village to sell for a couple of shillings each. But he was never going to get a mattress, let alone a TV or fridge by selling coconuts.

The next day as Hassan passed the wall, Idi called down to him: 'There's dollars for you too.'

'Yeah?' Hassan dropped the arms of his wooden barrow.

'He needs glass.'

'Glass?'

'Drinking glasses, soda bottles, whisky, whatever.'

Hassan leant against his barrow, with folded arms. 'Where would I get glass?'

'You take that,' Idi pointed at the barrow. 'Around the hotels. It's perfect for collecting glass.'

'You expect me to pay the deposit?'

'Tt,' Idi shook his head.

'To steal them?'

'Collect the broken ones.'

'He wants broken glass?' Hassan and Idi stared at each other for some time. 'You're mad brother. Why?'

Idi pointed up at the top of the wall separating the bumpy lane from the rich green trees beyond. His finger traced a range of high spiky mountains along the ridge of it.

When Idi heard a rattle coming along the coral-rag lane the next day, he began to mix cement. The orchestra grew louder as it passed through the scrub along the side of the wall that led to the beach. Idi could see from his perch on the wall how half Hassan's barrow was filled with the usual glossy green cases of coconuts, but the other half was flashing and sparkling in the sun.

'How's it going?' Hassan called up at Idi who was smearing the top of the wall with a thick dollop of cement.

17

'Cool.'

'Now what, brother?'

Idi pointed at the glass in the barrow and beckoned. 'Come on, give them here.'

Hassan picked at random the red metal cap and green neck of a Johnnie Walker bottle. He held it upside down, as if it were a ceremonial sword. A sharp shard of pointed glass rose from one side of the neck, ending in a jagged point. He saw the sun fill it, swirl around inside the neck, glint on the barbed peak.

'Quick, man, it's setting.' Idi beckoned again.

'Take care,' said Hassan.

'Get real.' Idi planted the bottle top firmly in the wet cement, its lethal point spearing upwards. 'Another. Hurry.'

Hassan selected one at a time and passed them up— the thick knobbly glass of deposit-only soda bottles that he had always thought impossible to break; clear spirit bottles; broken drinking glasses with stems. He'd seen tourists drinking from them, mixing the juice of fruits with spirits. They got pinker and laughed more, and then the girls slipped off, hand-in-hand with men, onto the night beach.

He watched silently as Idi worked his way along the wall that enclosed the birdful, fruitful, sweet-smelling garden.

He was still laughing when Idi told him to move the

18

ladder along the wall, and descended to join him. 'We need more glass.'

Hassan pointed at the sparkling crest of the wall. It made him think of the boys in town who competed to have the brightest and longest fringes on the back of their bicycle saddles, so as to be the coolest. He'd also heard of cooks at the hotels who were told to put leaves, and even flowers, on the plates of tourist food, with no expectation that they would be eaten.

He finally squeezed out: 'He pays you to make this?'

'Eheh.'

'Why?'

'You said you wanted dollars too,' said Idi. 'Why didn't you bring a full barrow?'

'But what does he want it for?'

Idi looked at the wall. 'He's made a beautiful place.'

'I remember,' said Hassan. 'But now no one sees it. Just the ornament.'

'Like you said. It's sharp.'

Hassan thought for a moment and looked up at the line of rising sharks' teeth. 'Does he keep animals? Monkeys perhaps, that he wants to eat, that mustn't escape?'

'No.'

'There must be something in there. Something that can climb so high.'

'Get more glass,' said Idi. 'We have the whole wall to do, beginning to end.'

The barrow changed its tune. It no longer rumbled past the wall each day with its rolling ripe coconuts, but approached with a distinctive jingle and chatter of glass that stopped somewhere along the foot of the wall, wherever Idi was with the cement.

Hassan got to know all the hotels on that part of the island, and went further and further to collect their breakages. Some of them had got wise to the demand and started to make a charge. And so he had become a businessman, calculating shillings against the dollars he would get at the end of the job, making trips later in the day for coconuts which would pay for the glass. He sent small boys for any shimmering scraps they could find in the sand at the edges of the hotel properties.

The glass nicked his fingers and sometimes it arrived at the wall sprinkled with blood. He bought gloves in the market. And he bought a pair of shades from someone he knew in town. They were scratched, but they looked cool. New York, New York, where all the chicks were, and dollars came from, and he supposed the man behind the wall, who he had never actually spoken to.

At nights, lolling on the *baraza*, the gathered boys would talk about their futures. Idi and Hassan bragged about the refrigerators that Eddie in town was going to fetch them from Dubai. One each, and an extra one for Idi's cousin. They'd seen photographs. They repeated the names of the special properties—freezer compartments, and thermostats, and ice cube makers. The other boys speculated on where they would gather glass the next day to sell on for shillings to Hassan the glass-entrepreneur.

'This one,' Hassan threw an arm over Idi's shoulder. 'He's going to be richest. He has dollars for two refrigerators.'

'Not yet,' said Idi.

'No?' Hassan winked at the other boys in the half light.

He lay there with the calculator in his hand. He would get a wife, a mattress, a fridge and a TV. In that order. Or maybe he would need the mattress before the wife. That was what he liked to talk about with the boys on the *baraza*, or think about as he drifted towards sleep.

Other conversation washed over him—the local politics that the boys teased apart; or the declining tuna catch and how it was linked to dynamite fishermen from the mainland who encroached on their patch and were wrecking the reef for the next generation; that low-slung car with the shaded windows that had appeared briefly and then flashed south again, and who it might belong to.

When the boys occasionally ran dry of subjects, the wall would sometimes resurface. But Hassan no longer thought much about why the man wanted it, the only wall on the whole island without rooms attached to it for people to shelter in.

'Wives,' one of the boys said. 'He has to stop them from running away.'

21

'Why do they run?' Another boy, laughing.

'Because he's too ugly.'

'Not rich enough.'

'Tt.' Heads were shaken in disbelief. They had never seen a single wife going in or out.

A new voice rose up in the dark—a boy visiting from the next village. 'What's it he's keeping out?' His laugh barked into the night. But Hassan barely heard the jabbering argument that followed.

Hassan and Idi worked their way around the enclosure, planting the glass. The fourth side was the beach, and remained open. Idi could see the man watching over it from his elevated terrace. The boys completed one side of the wall from beach to lane, then the other side. Then they started the last stretch along the lane itself. There was only one small section that they didn't decorate with glass—the big metal door at the entrance. The door had a tiny little slot that an *askari* peered through. But he barely grunted at them, never came out or chatted. He wore a uniform and had a kiosk in there, Idi said. He could see from the top of the wall. People said he came from the mainland, an ex-policeman.

'Sharp teeth,' said Hassan. 'They have sharper teeth on the mainland. Like the wall.'

With Hassan's glass foraging, and Idi's cementing, they were approaching the end of the job, the corner where the lane met with the wall coming up from the beach. The final barrow of glass chinkled in, and Idi filled the last gap with the pointed shard of a 7 Up bottle, still with a clean white logo on its side. Idi climbed down the ladder, and he and Hassan whooped and slapped hands.

'Now, rich-man brother,' said Hassan. 'You can give me my share of the dollars, right?'

'You'll get them. Sure,' said Idi.

The man was in the habit of walking his garden each day, to see that all was under control, prowling into the corners, inspecting, asserting his rule. Since the growth of the wall, there was less and less need to look for intruders over his shoulder, and no need to greet passers-by. The defences were complete and there was no one to see him. He was finally secure and singular.

He had woken that morning with a flutter of anticipation. What would he find flowering? He went out after the rain, closed his eyes and breathed in the garden's scents. As he walked the bounds, he found himself pausing to lay his cheek against the smooth cool flesh of a banana leaf, cup its purple bud between his hands. He even put his lips to the first petals of the frangipani bush. A kiss, almost.

He took a pair of secateurs with him, and a notebook and pencil to write instructions for the boy when he came in—what should be chopped or tidied, or brought into the house for a vase. He checked the shape of the bread-fruit tree; noted where a little tying-in would help the passion fruit vine to fan out further; decided which fruit to gather. 'Hibiscus,' he whispered to himself as he wrote. 'Prune. Use shears.' The words hissed out like a leaking hose in an English summer garden. Precious and slow. 'Billbergia nutans. Divide,' he wrote. He looked at the last word. How close it was to 'divine'. This brought a satisfying feeling.

But there was still some business to complete. The wall-boy had worked well, and had found glass for the top of it from somewhere. He had finished in good time, as he had promised, for his bonus. Now he deserved payment. The man would go to the safe as soon as the boy presented himself at the gate.

The ladder remained on the outside of the wall. As the final stretch of glass defence was now complete, he asked the *askari* to go out to the lane and retrieve the ladder from the boy. He had intended for it to be stored under lock and key at the entrance kiosk. But as he was studying a bougainvillaea newly planted against the wall, the *askari* approached, head down and sullen, lugging the ladder behind him.

At the same time, the man became aware of noise coming from the other side of the wall. This was nothing new. Usually it was people passing, and the noise passed with them. But he could hear slaps, and tinkles of glass. More than anything though, he could hear voices. They rose and fell, raw and throaty, too uninhibited to be harmless. And they didn't move on. He imagined a pack of men trying to burrow under the wall like wild dogs. He knew the diamond hardness of the coral rag, knew that this would be impossible, but still he pictured their raw scrabbling paws, snouts white with sand, drilling deep.

He pointed the *askari* to where he wanted the ladder against the wall and then dismissed him, back to the kiosk. He was a heavy man, some had even dared to suggest he was short, and he was unused to stairs. He dragged himself up the ladder, a step at a time, until he was eye-level with his sparkling battlements. His head burst suddenly out of the variegated shade into bright sunlight. The shock of harsh white light tipped his balance momentarily. Because of the dazzle, he didn't immediately see the gaggle of boys in celebratory mood. Nor did they at first notice him.

As his vision clarified, he saw the handcart, full of coconuts. He flinched as a *panga* came down with a long slow swing, thwacking on the skull-like fruit. He recognised the wall-boy he had employed. But he had insisted that the boy worked alone, and he'd never seen anyone else up on the wall. So who were all these others who lolled bare-chested and insolent, piratical in dark glasses? Each took a swig from the coconut, the backs of their hands swiping at their mouths afterwards. What was their intention—were they planning a raid and was this their pre-battle ritual?

25

He watched, made invisible by his stillness, wary of upsetting the balance of the ladder. His throat was hot, his legs beginning to tremble at being too high off the ground, his hands sweating on the ladder poles. He waited for signs of hostility, for weapons, or salutes or signals of aggression—for the gang to muster.

But the coconut passed between them with only laughter and a teasing kind of pushing and pulling at each other. A generosity of arms hung loosely around shoulders. Talk flicked up and down amongst them; a percussion of hand slaps. He watched.

And as he watched, a dam that had been shoring up a reservoir of memory gave way. A tide of laughter and chinking glasses. Bubbles of champagne snickering up his nose. A garden party on a lawn. She turned to smile at him. When she came over, he let her pick a strawberry seed from his lip before she linked his arm and they joined a new circle of friends and neighbours.

The ladder was buffeted by the current. He clung tighter to it.

The boys looked up at a rustling in the palm fronds and saw the pink face above the wall, as if it was impaled on a shard of glass, or as if the man was trying to escape from his own enclosure. Hassan saw something on the face, almost like embarrassment, like someone being caught doing something they were not supposed to do. A silence fell.

'Take him a coconut,' Idi hissed at Hassan. 'It's my boss.'
Hassan took up his *panga* again and thwacked open a
young fruit. He cut into it a drinking-sized hole and lifted
it up the wall, towards the man. 'You're welcome,' he said.

But without the ladder, Hassan was unable to reach
high enough and the man's hands were too low on the
other side of the wall.

'Take it,' said Hassan, grinning up at the pink confused
face, his arm at full stretch. And he saw the man lumber a
little against the wall, as if he might be trying to raise
himself far enough to lean over. But he stayed where he
was, at the same height.

'We're drinking to your wall,' said Hassan. 'It's
finished.'

The man gave a lop-sided grin or grimace and it looked
for a moment as if he would say something.

Taking his opportunity for the question he had almost
forgotten, Hassan asked, 'What is it for? The wall—the
glass.'

There was a moment of hesitation, a sideways glance.
Hassan turned to see smirks smearing one or two of the
faces behind him. And when he looked back, he thought
perhaps he understood the flicker of an answer crossing
the man's face.

He was sweating in the sun, and pressured by the height.
He looked back over his shoulder as if for the reassurance

of familiar territory, but the swaying movement of foliage behind him only cast his stomach like a buoy on waves. Half a dozen eager faces were peering at him. And they had asked him a question.

'It's . . .' he muttered. ' It's to . . .'

The boy with the coconut was smiling up at him, his arm outstretched. There was no malice in the face, but he could see that the smile was faltering, becoming less sure. It reminded him of being with his aunt. He had been sent away to stay with her for the holidays and she was pushing chocolate milk shake towards him in a posh London café. It was a treat and he knew he couldn't tell her that he felt sick. That would be rude. Instead he had vomited a brown sludge across the white tablecloth.

He hazarded a further step on the ladder, to get the height to reach over for it—the sweet juice offered to him by the smiling boy. But as his foot faltered onto the step, he felt the ladder wobble beneath him on the uneven ground, felt the need to descend to where he felt comfortable, to the soil and his dense green cover. He slipped backwards a little, arms and legs gecko-spread. The ladder felt too steep, as if it might peel back. There was no one there to hold it. Not on his side of the wall.

He saw the ladder arms lift and come towards him. A heart-throb-blinding stab of fear sent his hand forward to grab at something solid. He found purchase. His hand closed on the high sharp spear of a smashed Fanta bottle. The peak of his creation.

Blood sprang crimson bright, spurted in an arc over the spangled glass battlements and spattered onto the white ground beyond. A deep cut and gush reeled him backwards, so that he lost sight of the boys with their flickering grins, splashed back amongst the shiny leaves of his beautiful garden—his lagoon, saloon, the turquoise world of sea and sky that he now saw through sun-speckled foliage.

As his rich arterial blood flowed, he barely heard the chorus of cries led by Idi, 'Sir, sir!' as the boys found themselves truly walled out. He didn't hear footsteps running to the entrance, the battering against the metal gate and the appeals to the *askari* for his slow help.

His blood seeped in beads back into the earth and collected in pools on the glossy green leaves of the breadfruit tree that he had pulled down with him.

A Sense of Belonging

THEY WERE ALWAYS three. Because Kate's eyes followed the collie, she never noticed much about the couple, but she knew without looking that they dressed for the winter beach in big jackets, gloves and hats, and that they were always half smiling. She heard the laughter in their voices, and the woman's playful coaxing with the ball.

'Wait, Donny, wait. Yes, you can have it in a minute, you big . . . Isn't he a big. . . ? Go on then, boy'.

The couple came into focus momentarily when the dog flitted past them, weaving between them at a gallop. Against the black and white blur of him, she saw their legs, always in jeans. Her pink wellingtons with the swirling Gucci design. His well-worn Camel boots, sprinkled with sand.

She liked to watch as the dog went after the ball, his nose dropping to the ground as he approached it. But he was always going too fast. Despite his straight-legged braking, his body over-reached his nose, turning him almost into a somersault. It made her laugh out loud sometimes. Then he'd have the ball in his mouth, nose raised, eyes rolling back, a triumphal gallop to the shore. He'd skip through the shallows with an erect tail, on a still day stirring the gulls up from the placid glossy blue pools, then trot back to the couple to drop the ball at their feet again.

She knew that if she raised her eyes to the level of their faces when she passed them, they would be on 'good morning' nodding terms by now, but she preferred to whisper her inward greeting to Donny. She saved her smile for him. She longed to be able to play like that, unselfconsciously leaping and running and rolling and splashing. It reminded her of school days when she played rounders and hockey and cricket and there was always an excuse for red-cheeked animal exuberance. Being near the sea made her want to be like that again.

She could see the sea from the sitting room window of the flat she'd been renting since the summer—if she knelt on the table and pressed her cheek hard to the glass she could, anyway. She watched tankers and cruise ships and jet skis pass the horizon. She watched the world go by.

She liked to go to the beach every morning on her way to the bus, even in the winter, so she could gauge the day. She could see properly from there, rather than snatching at pinches of sky between buildings when she looked up

31

from the streets or from her flat. She never knew for sure whether a black bank of cloud was approaching on what seemed the brightest of days, hiding itself behind buildings. But on the beach with that flat, low tide brown slack of sand, and the blackened tarry groins stretching out towards the water, she knew she wasn't being deceived. She followed the curve of the bay to the Power Station in the south and its two huffing chimneys yellowing the sky, and in the other direction gazed at the pretty Fife villages facing her across the Firth. She could see a whole chunk of Scotland, the wide open sky, and knew what was coming for her day.

Between eight and nine each morning the promenade bristled with mothers with buggies. They accompanied the school kids who tight-rope-stepped the low wall above the beach, prompting the mothers' chorus, 'Get Down. Now!'. The kids dribbled balls, rode scooters, kicked debris which had blown up from the beach. They were pink-coated, squealing, hand-holding, chains of life and noise.

Their family lives were impenetrable to Kate. They mostly lived in the banks of tenements beyond the high wall separating promenade and beach. Someone had painted onto it, 'Wall, huh! What is it good for?' And the council hadn't yet painted over it, as if waiting for an appropriate answer first. Kate had one. It's good for keeping them beyond me, their alien lives, that's what it's good for, she thought.

Since she'd lived here, it was the people with dogs, not children, that jabbed at her and made her life seem incomplete. Every morning now when she passed the 'Donny three', with their commitment to each other, their homeliness worn like a heraldic shield, she felt herself rattling, a lone pebble on the beach. She avoided the grazes of other people's eyes on her as they walked their dogs. They seemed to think they owned the place.

In the summer there'd been an old lady she'd watched. Grey-haired and dark-glassed, she leant against the breakwater with her face to the sun, sandals off, her white Scottie waiting squarely for her nearby. It seemed that the dog gave her a right to be there on her own.

Sometimes she went to the beach at night when no one could see her, enjoying the blind crash of the waves which overpowered the sirens and the traffic hum of the city behind her. At the edge of the wet shore, a pale suggestion of lace spread and retreated. She could pretend she was somewhere very far away, in the Caribbean, even. Once when she'd been there at night, a voice and the heavy thud of running steps had loomed out of the murk, and a tall man in shorts and bare feet had bounded near to her, imitating the jibes and swings of his leaping dog. He was absorbed in a game with it. In the darkness the dog looked a kind of good-natured baskerville.

She noticed other combinations of dogs and people. One day, she saw a solitary man and a woman walking in opposite directions along the blustering beach, scarves horizontal. They'd just passed, and whilst they faced away from each other, their dogs—a terrier and a Jack Russell —had stopped and turned back, taut at the far reach of their leads and owners' arms, straining back towards each other. Legs trapezoid, the dogs were attracted without inhibition. Two days later she saw them tumbling together, off their leads. The man and the woman now walked side by side rather than away from each other, hands in pockets, heads bent deep in conversation.

Her eye for cameos of beach life eventually brought her the answer. It was a man who walked the shore, way up the far wild end, where factories and warehouses back onto the promenade. The tractors didn't go that far up the beach in the mornings to rake the sand. Green-streaked rocks surfaced from beneath it, forcing their way through the Victorian seaside facade. The man was way down by the shore, striding parallel with it. Periodically, his arm uncoiled in a throwing motion—rhythmically, regularly. However long she squinted into the winter light, she could not see stick or ball, nor the dog that his movement suggested, retrieving and returning it to him. She supposed it was a dog of memory or imagination that accompanied him, that he so convincingly had choreographed. His movements gave him a sense of belonging to the beach though, and no one except her seemed to have noticed the absence of the animal itself.

On her way to the bus she marched down the street that ran parallel to the beach—contrasting the sea's brightness with a gloom of high, grey Victorian buildings. Shops spilled stepladders, cheap garden furniture, and premature Christmas decorations onto the pavements. She went into the pet shop and she bought a firm, bouncable, solid red rubber ball.

The next morning she set the alarm earlier than usual and went straight down to the beach, onto the sand, hands out of her pockets, the ball ready. She felt the excitement along the nerve and muscle of her arm as she threw it the first time. She hesitated, then ran after it, scooping it up as Donny did, still at a run, spraying sand into her shoes so she felt the crunch under the sole of her foot, in her sock.

In the distance, way behind her, she heard a high call, 'Donny, Donny, here! Come here!' Insistent and repetitive. She ignored it, threw the ball again, ran towards it. And then she became aware of competition next to her, sand churning under his paws, wide-eyed, his neck stretched desperately forward, mouth panting and open. She laughed, ran faster, faster than she could remember moving since she was a kid. She launched herself towards the ball on the ground, but she was too slow. Donny had it in his teeth, and was galloping his victory parade with it while she lay sand-sprawled in her office clothes. She got up and ran after him again, then stopped and looked around. Two figures, one in pink wellingtons, trailed way behind them, not even running. She watched Donny flicking spray up in the shallows, launching gulls into the sky.

'Donny.' She quavered a thin, experimental cry. He looked towards her. Not towards his owners. 'Come on then, boy.' She bent forward slightly, slapped her thighs. And then he was trotting towards her with his mouth slavering on the ball. He dropped it at her feet, retreated several paces, never taking his eyes from the ball, unbreathing, watchful. His front legs were stretched in front of him, head low, tail high. And then just for a second, he let one eye flicker briefly to her face, a question asked by the squint of his ears.

She cast a quick glance over her shoulder, picked up the ball, and threw it far along the beach towards the warehouses and factories, with her almost forgotten cricketer's length and range, her flaccid arms twanging with lack of practice.

Donny ran away from the pink wellingtons and the invisible sand-coloured Camel boots, towards the ball, and she ran after him, feet slipping on the sand, heart bumping, leg muscles pinching. They ran together towards the far wild end of the beach. Kate's lungs rasped as she ran, with the exertion and with the bellows of laughter that erupted from her, over and over.

Neither of them looked back.

Staying in Lane

LATER, TINA WOULD blame it on 'Larry'—as the badge on his shirt had labelled him—for getting too close, for starting something. With their knees almost touching, his breath carried a suggestion of heat and mint, and she had felt the prickle of proximity. It reminded her of how slow dances at school discos had tricked her body into a response just because she was close enough to smell someone, to feel their heart beat. It happened even with the ugliest boys. Her face would be tucked over their shoulder so she couldn't actually see them. All they seemed to need was a pulse.

She would admit Larry's role later. But at the time there was just a feeling of faint embarrassment, and an awareness of a small patch of stubble on his right cheek that he had missed when shaving. She concentrated on that rather than the almost-brush of his knee on hers as she stared at a hot air balloon at the end of a long straight road, and answered his repeated question: 'Better or worse?' Then he had turned the light out and come eye to eye with her, with just a torch between them. She was aware of little more than his breath amplified in her right ear, the red veins at the back of her own eye, and the rustling of his clothes as he stretched across her. Her hands rested, sweaty, on her thighs.

'Better give you a new prescription, I think.' The room lights had came back on as he settled back with a slight creak to his crisp white shirt, the sleeves folded to the elbow, blond hairs on an early tan. 'Need to be able to read the road signs if you're going up and down that big bad road across the border.'

'They've changed, then?' she said. 'My eyes.'

'Age, I'm afraid.' And then he was ushering her out of his small windowless cell back into the sun-splashed showroom, one hand hovering at the base of her back. She was glad he couldn't see the outrage in her face.

She chose the new frames quickly. If her sister had been with her, or her flamboyant friend Rosanna, there would have been more of a parade in front of the mirror, but she felt a need to get out of there, onto the road, to start the long journey ahead. And anyway, who looked at you when you were driving, unless you were one of the new breed of middle-aged women taking to convertibles. *Woman's Hour* had done a feature on it. The presenter had emphasised that you had to be confident of yourself, prepared to be looked at, to drive a convertible. Tina might as well go for the cheapest option when it came to new glasses.

Later, she would also come to blame the optician's assistant, 'Shirley'. She'd been clicking her decorated nails on the till buttons when she piped up, 'There's an offer, you know. Did you know that? On sun specs. Another pair —prescription ones, like—free.'

'Oh?' Tina beat down the instinct to grab the bag containing the £29 brass-framed pair and get out of the shop. It was just politeness really that stopped her. Shirley was already half way across the floor on her pink heels, waving at a rack of frames on the wall.

'These are all in the offer. Lovely styles this year, don't you think? The celebrity look,' she ran a finger up and down them. '"Munro".' Shirley held up a cat-eyed pair rimmed with purple. 'Gorgeous, aren't they. Or are you more of a Hepburn? The classic look.'

Tina remained gripped by the floor.

'These are great—sort of 'Thelma and Louise', eh?' Shirley pointed at a brown-lensed pair with a clear curvaceous rim.

'"Monster Dog",' Tina muttered.

'Sorry?'

'I don't think I could wear glasses called "Monster Dog".'

'Oh. Right. Or "Posh",' Shirley flicked the hair from her

shoulder in a Posh-like gesture and pulled out a wrap-around version. 'Glamorous, eh?'

Was she serious—Tina glamorous? Wanting to look like Audrey Hepburn or Posh Spice?

The optician—Larry—was wheeling a girl in a backless dress into his small dark room, head bent towards hers in a gesture of courteous over-interest. The first show of sun and yards of skin exploded from under the dust sheets at this time of year. The girl probably had twenty-twenty vision anyway, at her age. As Larry guided the girl through the doorway, he smiled back into the showroom at the transaction going on between Tina and Shirley. Tina was sure, and immediately afterwards doubted, that Larry had winked at her.

'Up to you,' Shirley shrugged, discouraged perhaps by Tina's lack of response. She started to move back towards the till.

Tina snatched at the cat-eyed 'Munro' pair. 'I'll take these,' she said, and then feeling she needed a reason, 'I hate squinting when I'm driving. It's dangerous.'

~

Once out of the city and onto the winding A-roads, she relaxed, finding relief in getting going, even though progress was slow, and the inside of the car too hot. She passed the familiar sign, BOARDING KENNELS AND

CAT RESORT. Maybe it was the sun today, or the new prescription spectacles sharpening everything up, but the sign set off her imagination as if it was the first time she'd seen it. She conjured up cats stretched out on the poolside, purring in their skimpy bikinis and shades—Munro style perhaps—a straw dangling between mouth and cocktail glass. It was a cat's life. The dogs only got to 'board'.

She found that she was still smiling about it when lights stopped her for some road works. When they changed to green, a row of half-smiling workmen wearing fluorescent jackets and helmets leant on their tools and nodded the traffic by. The men seemed slowed from their usual industry by the unexpected warmth. It was almost as if it made a holiday for them, a break from routine, the news that there would be a summer this year after all. She felt as if something might leap from her through the windscreen towards them, especially that one taking his helmet off as if to sweep her through. What was it that wanted to leap—a song? Or just a slightly longer enjoyment of that smile? But she was serious again—she had to concentrate on the road ahead. Ever the careful driver.

Soon there were only remnants of familiar landmarks —a hill that she'd helped dig up on an archaeology field trip long ago, near Lanark, with a name she couldn't recall; the turn off to a pink hotel where there had been a christening or some other family event. Her sister had arrived on the arm of that Italian stallion—all hand gestures and bulges in embarrassing places.

And then Tina was on the M74, heading south for Cumbria. She turned the radio on, settling in for the main stretch of her journey.

Driving a road like the M74 was like being in an airport —you were in transit, not quite in one world or the other. You weren't tied to any sense of self, until the pieces of you had to fall back into place as you neared your destination a few hours later.

The sun was lowering in the sky, edging towards the high backs of the southern uplands which were dotted with sparkling white lambs. Although she pulled down the sun-shade, she was still squinting. It was then that she remembered the sun specs in their case stuffed out of sight in the glove compartment.

It was hard to say whether it was wearing the new shades —she leant towards the rear-view mirror again to catch the full effect—or the soundtrack provided by changing from Radio 4 to 2. But when she looked at the dials, she was doing ten miles per hour more than usual. She was speeding. But the road was emptying except for trucks snaking towards England. It was too early in the year for holiday traffic, and commuters were already home. It was quite safe, quite easy driving, you barely needed to concentrate.

She tipped her head back a bit, settled into her seat so that her arms were straight at the wheel, ruffled her hair, and turned the radio up a notch. A smile whiskered onto her face, as 'Keep on Running' came on. Stevie Winwood had provided the soundtrack when she was twenty.

Sunshine was good for you, she'd read that in a book. People were aroused by it too, the book said. Men, she had assumed. And now her car was full of it—sunshine pouring through the windscreen and pooling in her lap. She felt like a cat on a windowsill, stroked and glossed into an ecstasy.

A blue van passed her. It's company spiel on the back said, FIFTEEN SUCCESSFUL ERECTIONS PER DAY! They were going for cheap laughs. A scaffolding company. But she almost did laugh. She bumped across the cat's eyes to overtake a line of trucks. A row of thick bare arms were displayed in the open drivers' windows above her: tattooed and orange-tanned by the low sun; no faces attached.

Then a black Golf was ahead of her, in the slow lane. She passed it, noticing as she approached that there was a face framed in the driver's wing mirror. Once ahead, she could look straight into the car. If the driver had been picking his nose, or singing along to Gloria Gaynor, or crying even, she could have seen. Driving wasn't so very private after all.

A suggestion of striped T-shirt in the reflection was enough to make her wonder if he was the man who had held the door open for her at the petrol station. As they'd passed in the doorway she'd noticed how his T-shirt had been taut across his chest, looser just beneath, giving a suggestion of his body shape. Their eyes had snagged briefly and it had sent her hand to her cheek, wondering if she had left a smear of sandwich on it.

Was 'Keep on Running' playing in his car too?

The hills either side of the M74 seemed greener than she'd ever seen them, the lambs whiter. Perhaps that was what wearing shades did for you. Made the world look different. She had to remind herself to look at the road too.

A few miles further, on a downhill stretch, the black Golf overtook her. She'd seen it coming in her wing mirror, and deliberately stared ahead as they levelled, her mouth pursed, just in case he looked, just to prove what it was she had her mind on.

But when she pulled in front of him the next time, over the bump between lanes, she gave the wheel a slight flick, like the kink of your hips when you ski or skate. A flick that suggests youth and sexiness and agility. It was funny how you could make a car do that too. Like a dance. She had the mirror advantage now, could see the whole of his windscreen. And although his face jumped and vibrated a bit, she could see that he was smiling straight at the back of her head, or at the post-box strip of her eyes he could probably see in her rear-view mirror. Her Munro eyes. Thank you, Larry, she thought.

That tiny unshaved patch on the optician's cheek. It dredged back into her memory a man whose raw stubble had brushed against her neck and sent shivers through her, like electricity down a cat's tail. There had been other would-be lovers who'd had that effect too—one whose slightly calloused workish hands had found their way under her clothing as they danced, resting at the base of her hot back. They had been identical heights so that everything matched when she turned to him, so that the kiss was inevitable. And he'd whispered a mantra in her ear, 'I want to lick your pussy'. She blushed to think of it.

A terribly bad film last night—she hadn't really watched it but snatched glimpses of as she was packing—had made her wonder how her own thighs might feel to someone else through nothing but silk. Her nipple itched against a new, too-stiff bra. The wink of the optician, the T-shirted chest of the petrol station man, that kiss that had nearly blown from her lip to hand to air when she passed the workmen at the traffic lights. (Gosh—so it had been a kiss). She felt like one of those balsa wood planes with an elastic band that you twisted and tightened as a kid. A notch at a time. She should watch out then. When you released the plane, as far as she recalled, it would spring into the air, fluttering in a scattered frenzy this way and that, only to crash sometime later.

She fidgeted in her seat. Her clothing had somehow ruckled beneath her, and as she squirmed away from it, a rumble of road surface vibrated up through the axle of her car. She veered, rather suddenly, off the hard shoulder, and back into lane.

The soundtrack beat on. 'I Heard it on the Grapevine' and then inevitably, Marvyn Gaye crooning 'Sexual Healing'. The volume in her car was so loud that the speakers rattled and distorted. She sang along, the Diva that she was, as the game of leap frog continued—the natural, or perhaps intentional, cycle of slowing and increasing speed.

She was in the middle lane, and the black Golf came alongside on her right. It stayed level longer than usual. She was a woman with forty-five years' experience in the body of a twenty-year old, sophisticated and in control, in her Munro shades. They were neck and neck and she was laughing. Laughing out loud. She turned her head to the right, to face him, turned back to look at the road, just late enough to see his head turning too and the snatch of it back to face ahead. She turned again. Their smiles connected this time, before they both looked back at the road. 'You Sexy Thing' came on. Her lips were moist around the words and she pouted them out, sang along. And then she turned, met his gaze and mouthed the words, 'Dirty Boy', with no idea where or why they came from her.

She saw shock on his face and his hunched laughter, and then she crunched down a gear and accelerated ahead. The rumble of cat's eyes warned up through the floor, followed by a screech of brakes behind, a horn blasted so close it seemed to be in the car with her. She swung back to the right to avoid the van in the slow lane, but swung too far, bumped into the fast lane towards the central reservation, heard brakes again, veered left, weaving dangerously now. A black car was very, very close. The middle lane again. Recovering. Going straight. Red-faced. Her heart with the wings of a humming bird.

~

She turned off the engine once she had found a space in the service station car park, and called her sister. It seemed suddenly very quiet without the radio on. Her heart was still going a bit too fast, her hands a little shaky.

The sun was just disappearing behind the haunches of the uplands. Only another hour and a half she told her sister, and yes, she'd brought marmalade and bread for breakfast, and she thought they would be able to negoti-ate Mother's wheelchair down the gravel path and onto the road. And of course it was OK that her sister wouldn't get there till the morning—Tina was well aware of the nature of her social life. And no, there wasn't anything wrong. She had just had a bit of a close shave, that was all.

She climbed out of the sun-caged car. The sky was still clear and blue above her but the air was cold now, the sun gone, a wind whipping across the car park to curl her shoulders. Colours dusked back to grey as she removed the Munro shades, no longer needed. She leant into the car to pull out her brown overcoat, her remnant of winter, and noticed it was covered in dog hair. Which was strange. She didn't even have a dog.

She gave it a couple of brushes and shrugged it on. Just then, a black Golf swept into the car park. Heat flushed upwards from her feet into her face. The car swooshed to a halt two parking places away. How was it she hadn't noticed on the road that it had a sunshade stuck to the rear window with 'Pooh' inscribed on it and a picture of a bear gorging from a honey pot?

Before he could get out of his car, she turned her rounded, brown-coated back and bustled towards the shelter of the service station toilets.

Angel Face

'So, WHERE DID you get this?' Alec picked up a head from where it lay on Tom's workshop floor amongst coils of chain, steel brackets, a redundant ring gear and a starter motor.

'Skip. Behind Makro's,' said Tom, wiping white paint down his boiler suit leg.

Alec cupped the head in his hands. It had beigey-orange flesh tones and a cleanly machined amputation at the neck. 'Wanted someone to talk to—that it?'

Tom took the head out of Alec's hands, stood it on the plastic-sheeted block, pulled his mask back down, and took aim with the paint gun. Alec noticed how he was careful not to spray too heavily, avoiding drips. The head turned white, hair and all. Alec found it hard with its new, eerie finish, to imagine it on display in the window of the local clothes store, parading on its missing body some daft shell suit. Like the red one he'd seen last week, with the white trim, labelled 'For your seasonal flight of fancy—only £9.99'.

He looked away, stood for a moment shaking his head, then stomped back to the canteen. Tom was away with the fairies. He never joined the boys at lunchtime these days for the ricochet of dirty jokes and crossword clues through the smoke and coffee fumes. He stayed in his workshop with his lunch-box propped open behind him, eating as he messed about with his useless, ugly constructions. And now it seemed he was spending his nights scrabbling around in skips behind the arcade.

He'd better watch it, that's all. Alec had seen Nina's pinched, crabbit face glaring after Tom from their doorway. She'd never exactly been a beauty queen, right enough. But these days she was chewing lemons. He knew trouble when he saw it—the shadow of a silent battle raging between her and Tom. A battle Tom maybe didn't even know about.

When Alec passed the workshop again after his lunch, Tom was gazing at the white head, hands on his hips. Alec caught sight of a long straight nose, and hooded eyes that now seemed naked of lashes and pupils.

He'd seen people standing like Tom—in the museum when he'd taken the kiddies that time. Lost and absorbed in front of paintings. Look, look, look. They'd made him want to laugh. All that looking.

'What flavour is it anyway?' he shouted at Tom, making

him jump. 'Male or female?'

'Never really thought,' Tom turned his gaze back to the head.

'And, eh . . . what's it for?'

But Tom didn't hear him above the clank and wheeze of the machines being started up again after lunch. Or he didn't answer anyway.

∼

Alec noticed in the following days how the head watched over the workshop from the bench, silent and serious, while Tom painted other bits and pieces in his lunch-hours. He'd welded together an upright T-frame taller than himself. Lengths of drive chain were now draped side by side over the horizontal bar to make a dense sheet which reached to the floor. Then he sprayed it white. From a distance you just saw a waterfall of white, not the chain at all. But he'd wrecked it. The parts would never move again with that paint seizing up the plates and rollers. Alec wondered if the boss knew.

Flat on the floor Tom had coiled some chain within the outline of two lozenge-type shapes. He'd fixed the chain rigid. Painted them too. Now he was spraying a ring gear, taking care to penetrate the paint deep between the teeth.

Alec hovered nearby, waiting. Tom eventually turned off the gun and pulled up his mask.

'Got all the bits now, Alec. Just need to assemble it.'

'Into what?'

'See this,' he indicated the ring, 'this is going to be the . . .'

'Christ's sake, man.' Alec's frustration barked across Tom's explanation.

'Well if you're not interested . . .'

'What do you want me to do—burst out in fairy lights?' Alec watched Tom clearing up, presumably preparing to resume his paid work. 'Do you not need your job anymore?'

'Course.'

'And what about Nina?'

'Nina?'

Alec felt himself fumbling, something child-like rising behind his eyes, connected to the angry knot in his stomach. 'Look,' he said. 'Look.'

Tom frowned.

'Look,' Alec tried to lay the words down calmly, to breathe. 'It's that long since we've had a pint together. How about the Cross Keys later, eh?'

Tom was wide-eyed. 'I was going to ask you a favour.'

'Eh?'

'About your pick-up. Any chance of a hand tonight, a lift? With your pick-up?' Tom's smile smoothed his face, licked it into a mesmerising grace. 'Then a pint, eh?'

It was a heavy, lumpen thing to shift. Tom had wrapped it in sacking. He insisted they move it out of the workshop like it was a fragile baby, not a ton of steel. It was too much for them really, just two of them. Tom had the look of a man on a secret mission as he directed Alec onto the M8. It was clear that questions weren't permitted.

'Pull in here,' Tom indicated the hard shoulder. 'Where that sign is. With the up-light.'

Alec flashed a glance sideways, but Tom's face in profile gave away only an inner glow. Alec cursed to himself and braked hard. They heard the thing in the back slide and bump towards them.

'What now?'

At a command from Tom, a gut-wrench of a lift, they slid the sack-clothed thing upright and slid its base plate onto a three-foot high black block that just happened to be on the edge of the hard shoulder. With his nose up against it, Alec smelt the workshop—the peary smell of paint, and the machine oil that clung to everything. Passing traffic slashed through the frost-bitten air, strobe lighting them through the central reservation. Tom was already fixing bolts between the base and the plinth with a powered wrench. Alec could see he'd chosen the position so that light from the sign sprayed up onto the 'thing', now towering above them.

He perched on the tailgate, in a haze of his own breath,

wishing he'd brought gloves. He thought ahead to the fug of the Cross Keys, and a pint in front of him. The daft escapade would be worth it when he could get Tom's attention, bend his ear.

Tom pulled the stepladder from the back of the pick-up and climbed up, slashing the bindings, and finally tugging off the sacking.

Alec's body jerked as if in electric shock. He stood up.

Suddenly above him hung a thing of light, with wings. A fully-fledged luminous angel. It had a halo, and a face— what a face—looking down at them. A long straight nose, full lips and downcast eyes. It took him a moment to equate this spectacle with the heavy mess of painted metal he thought he knew was under the sacking. You'd have to call it beautiful. Grace. That was the word spreading its wings in his mind.

Tom climbed down to him.

'Where did you get the face?'

'I told you. Out the skip.'

'But . . . that's an angel's face, is it no?'

'Aye. It is now. Just like the ring gear's a halo.'

They drove to the next intersection and then doubled back to drive past again. They saw the angel from miles off, hovering luminously three feet above the ground. Tom had to summon Alec's attention back to the road, he was so intent on looking at it, getting another glimpse of that face and its—whatever it was—before they passed.

'Put your foot down, man,' said Tom. 'You'll have the polis onto us—going under thirty on a motorway'.

It looked to Alec as though its wings would any minute sweep it away and up above Glasgow's winter smog halo. That was the one thing he knew about angels. They didn't hang about for long.

A few days later a photo appeared in the *Evening Times*, taken at night. 'Mystery angel lands on M8,' said the caption.

At the Christmas party, Alec caught sight of Nina's face, shrink-wrapped, her shoulders folding in. He found his moment.

'Have you seen this, Nina?' He held out the newspaper, folded to show the photograph of the hovering angel.

'Aye, they're all asking where it came from. Who did it. It's not the council.'

'It's not.'

Nina looked up at Alec, hearing some sort of authority in his voice.

'Look close to home, Nina.'

Alec headed for his next beer. He passed Tom who was walking towards Nina, holding out a gin and tonic, the bubbles fizzing on a slice of lemon. When Alec looked over his shoulder, he saw that Nina's face was lifting up, opening, unpeeling a question into Tom's face.

Glitter

THE MEN WERE in the road outside the pub kicking something on the ground. The kicks were muted into scuds and scuffles by the dense blanket of soft new snow. Standing in a pool of orange streetlight, Jeanie's breath froze.

The door of the pub gaped a square of artificial light and silhouetted figures. Shouts spilled out, and jukebox squeals. The surrounding hills had become stalking and unfamiliar, glossed with moonlight, drawn closer to the village centre so that they seemed to leer over what the men were doing.

Having come to the pub straight from their work on the hills or building sites, the men still wore their steel toe-capped boots. They were ice-hard. Their strikes made a 'flump' of impact. When the floored man stopped groaning at each kick, the impact started to sound wet.

Jeanie could imagine the fuse line of small events which had stilled pub conversation, and swivelled drinkers' heads. It had probably started with an

56

accidental jostle, and then a raised voice—an excuse for a backlog of irritation to be released. One word was enough, or perhaps two, 'ye cunt', and then the flat of hand on a chest, a shattering of glass, a crowd shrinking back, a tumble of battling bodies leaving cigarette smog for the snowy street.

It was a fuse line that transformed red-faced jokers into killers. She winced at each blow. It was the kind of kicking she had recently received herself from brutal words.

She vomited onto the snow.

Jeanie knew that the men would be gone the next morning, but the snow would remain. Frozen overnight into a crystalline sheet, it would be stained red and opaque in the centre, pink at the edges. Later, sparks of sun would edge upwards as day pushed the hills back onto their haunches. The red patch would melt. The kids, herded across the road by Rita Macintosh, would point at it as raspberry slush-puppy. Before they returned in the afternoon, the snow plough would come through and remove the evidence.

In this village she had watched children grow into young men and women. Some rode horses for silver cups, or danced at Sadler's Wells. There was always the glitter of laughter in the streets. From her corner at the crossroads, clutching her fluorescent lollipop, Rita Macintosh's marionette arms rose and fell for the drivers of familiar cars each morning. She sang out greetings for pedestrians

—'Morning, Joan' and 'Hello, Mr Morrison'. This was a place where doors were left unlocked, and pots of jam stewed from garden fruit left on doorsteps.

She saw now the thin disguise of the village, the shape-shifting that made the hills blaze with golden gorse in a summer sunset, but flash to a black glower in a new slant of light. Men who bent to chuck a child's chin were also booted monsters. The village had snashed its icicled teeth, and spat gobbets of frozen blood.

Under the streetlight, on a snowy pavement, tasting vomit, she felt the urge to run away. She wanted to be somewhere with no delusions, where no one expected anything of each other. Where she could be invisible.

'If you ever need it,' a friend had said, 'the flat's there. Somewhere else to be.'

She put on her running shoes. Like a streak of fox, she turned her back and slunk away.

Her fists pumped up ahead of her, leaving the collective kicks of the village behind. Her stride became long and sure, her breath coming easier. She had tamed the temptation to look behind.

Through glens and over hills, she padded along the white track laid by moon and snow. A rhyme started to rattle in her head against the blurred vibration of her vision. Its rhythm pounded with her feet.

The fox went out on a chilly night

He prayed for the moon to give him light
For he'd many a mile to go that night
Before he reached the Town-o!
Town-o! Town −o!

Dawn came ice-blue. An occasional car purred past, kicking up snow in soft patters behind it. Sunlight stabbed through trees. When she looked into the forest, the lover was there in the form of a tall birch, looking solid and dependable. She left it behind. When the tears tried to come, she locked them in. You cannot run and cry. Just as, she'd discovered, you cannot make love and cry. Each demands the body totally.

Like a dance, like a dive into deep water, like the swinging attack of a boot, running proved she was alive. She also knew that it would build her an armour of gun-metal muscle. There would be no nick of softness into which a knife could be forced.

She stopped to breathe, dabbing at the snow with one toe. Long ago her mother told her that there were crystals in snow. In the garden she had searched for diamonds, precious stones, treasure, running towards a cluster of rubies gleaming on a white bed. But when she'd gathered them in her hand, she found they were just hawthorn berries, and the disappointment had jerked tears from her.

'They're still beautiful,' her mother had said.

'Not jewels,' she had stamped at the hard snow.

'And these aren't pearls,' her mother had scooped a teardrop from Jeanie's face onto the end of her gloved finger. 'So put them away.'

On the road a magpie pecked at the glistening entrails of a rabbit. One for sorrow. Another magpie sparkled up black and white from the bushes. They joined forces and went at it from either side until a passing car swooshed them back.

She ran again.

He did not mind the 'quack quack quack'
And their legs all dangling down-o
Down-o! Down-o!

The city drew near. She flashed past doorways, lamp-posts, the corners of buildings. She saw her own reflection in a shop window, strung-out and loping, softer-looking than she wished, her hair flashing in the sun as it bounced. The landmarks of the half-familiar neighbourhood came up at her. The pub on the corner with its window-full of people with dark shadows under their eyes who wore ill-fitting shoes, and too-thin clothes for the temperature. The red van that was always parked up, with a promise on its side: 'World Conquerors Christian Corps —for miracles and healing'. Steam gushed from a wall like dragon's breath.

A left turn, and she was there.

It was a relief to be somewhere else. Here in the city, she could get up late, and leave her curtains drawn. She could choose to speak to no one except cashiers, and even that could be avoided with automatic checkouts.

The city expected violence of you. It was natural. In the stairwell, when she came in one day, a man was propped against the wall, his belly bulging into the corridor, eyes still and pupil-less with drink. She had to pass him, her chest still heaving from her daily run, limbs tingling. Her right hand flexed, making a fist. It longed to plunge through blubber towards the man's back bone. She restrained it in her jacket pocket.

After the Bellyman, she saw no one in the tenement. She only heard, each morning before seven, a member of the Italian family from the ground floor flat, climb to the top of the building to take their revenge on slovenly neighbours by sweeping the length of the stair, knocking the broom against every corner of masonry and clonking their heels on the hard steps. There were strange quietnesses and bass beats that murmured from unidentifiable sources in the building. Outside, abrupt skylines threw shadows across the pavements.

Her days were a shock of white and blue. Running gave them a structure. She got thin and light. Not like a butterfly's wing, but like grass that thrashes in the wind on a mountainside. Her hands felt scaly as lizard skin. She didn't look in the mirror, but imagined her hair steely, her face tight.

When she went back to the flat each day, she poured water into a long glass and sucked its bite onto her raw stomach lining. Snow, she thought. Water is just melted snow. When she held the glass against the white glare of window, the water became invisible. But she had also seen water blue and black to match the sky. Water was ungraspable, slithering down a drain like a snake's tail, as impossible to hold onto as the lover who turns away a smiling face and presents his back instead.

She ran towards a noise. She was on the Links, where the orange and purple crocuses were piercing the snow, their colours muted by the dusk. The cry was guttural, like an animal in pain. There was a flumping noise that made her stomach flinch. But it excited her too. Attracted and repelled, she ran towards it and away, carving a zigzag path into the snow.

Eventually she saw that the sound came from a boy in a duffel coat. He scooped an armful of snow into a slabby ball that he held in one open hand. The other hand, poised above his head, flat and knife-edged, powered downwards with that feral cry and sprayed snow all around him.

The next day, where the boy had been stood, a snowman with a pot belly and a red scarf. Two currants peered from an otherwise featureless face. She stood still, like an opponent, daring it. And then her elbow was up behind her, fist plunging hard into the gut. The snow gave a little beneath her knuckles and she felt the washboard tension in her own body.

She ran fast now, her lungs stinging with gulps of icy laughter.

John, John, the grey goose is gone
And the fox is on the town-o
Town –o! Town- o!

She ran out across the plain. There should have been a horizon or a slope leading up to hills. Instead there was a row of town houses, a sandstone school with black railings, a high fence surrounding allotments. She missed the hills. But not their conspiracy.

Illuminated faces beat her back through the city. Faces through glass, hands on pints. People contained by shut doors. There were so many pubs in a city. Each one could burst at any moment, throwing out a knot of tumbling men, with boots to splatter something wet and dark onto the white streets.

The next day a deep frost turned snow into rock. Out on the Links, she saw the duffel-coated boy return to his snowman with a carrot. However hard he pushed it into the ungiving face, to try and give the man a nose, it made no impression. So the boy lifted his elbow and knocked off the whole boulder-head of the stupid snowman and left it in two pieces on the ground.

Inwardly, Jeanie cheered.

The days continued to glitter with blue and white and sparkling low sunlight. One day as she ran down the street where the red van parked, she saw something on the rear shelf of a blue Merc. It blazed so brilliantly that she had to look away to protect her eyes. A gold casket, burnished and incandescent. She puzzled why it had not attracted a crowd. Perhaps it was only her that could see it? She imagined the back of the red van flying open to disgorge armoured Christian Conquerors on horseback. They raised their hands to make water into wine, one fish into a meal for a thousand. She went home feeling as if she had at last found treasure, and in such an unexpected place.

She slept. Night soothed her muscles, and her enemies paraded past, laying their cold hands on her stomach, and asking for compassion.

The next day the snow changed again. Clouds had gathered; the glint of winter sun vanished. Warm winds rushed in and everything dripped.

When she got to the Merc, she saw that without the sun illuminating it, the casket on the rear shelf was plastic —a fake-gold encrusted tissue box. Her miracle was an optical illusion. She stared at the piece of trash from Pound Stretcher. She stared at a knot of people who she now saw outside the pub on the corner, gathered around something on the ground, no doubt something they were trying to kill. And she ran the other way.

She stamped and kicked at the last traces of snow. It

was mostly air, she realised. Snow appears to be something of weight and substance, colludes with sun or moonlight to grow hills into mountains, transform Leith Links into a Mongolian plain. A belief in the grandeur or substance of snow was as deluded as believing she was alive just because her feet moved, and her lungs rasped. A belief that people cared about each other or were kind or good because they waved or smiled or knew each others' names, or asked, 'how are you?' She might as well believe that Christians on horseback, a whole cavalry of them, would save her. After all, the red van never moved, just parked itself in a shadowy side-street with its doors closed.

Jeanie knew all about illusions. What had looked like love was nothing of the sort. It was just the sparkle glued to a Christmas card that falls off when you brush it.

She ran and ran.

But when she came back down the street two hours later, the knot of people outside the pub was still there. In fact, there were more of them. Men in overalls, straight from work, were kneeling around something. She stopped running and edged towards the mob. no one would notice her.

One man broke away from the huddle, and she heard him on a mobile phone.

'I'll be late,' he said. 'Something's come up. It's urgent, aye. Life or death, actually.'

A child's fishing net lay fluorescent on the ground next to the steel toe-capped boots of a man on his stomach, stretched towards a drain. The cover had been lifted off and cast aside. As she came closer, leant in with the others, she saw that he was scattering a grainy dust into the pool of diesel-streaked meltwater that ran below the city streets.

'Come on, dear,' a woman stirred the water with a stick. 'He's gone again, eh?'

There was a collective gasp as Jeanie saw a flash of dull orange flicker just below the surface. A flutter of excitement. 'There he is,' they murmured. 'There he goes.'

The steel-toe-capped man turned to reach for the net. Jeanie smelt whisky on his breath. He scooped the net through the drain, raising it to look at its contents every now and again.

The door to number 18 opened and a woman came out with a tray of rising steam—steam that materialised into mugs as she lowered it to the pavement. She looked up with a smile and Jeanie turned away, ready to run.

'Would you like one, dear? It's no bother, really. I've one extra.'

Jeanie turned back, cleared a stone of ice from her throat, met the woman's smile. 'What is it?' she asked. 'What's everyone doing here?'

'It's a goldfish dear, got itself into a spot of bother.'

Jeanie looked around the circle of faces opening towards her.

'A goldfish?'

The woman with the tray nodded and smiled again.

In swam a childhood image—a goldfish held up to the sunlight in a bag, glinting its orange scales to earn its name. The woman handed her a mug.

Jeanie listened in to the phone calls to the water and sewage department, the fire service, the SSPCA. Sugar was stirred, and rescue tactics discussed. The man with the mobile phone delayed his meeting again. The pub window was studded with concerned faces. A steel toe-cap kicked over the pot of fish food, and a man with a crooked gold-toothed smile handed around cigarettes. All this for the murky dull flash of an orange fish, she thought.

She saw that the woman from number 18 was still smiling at her. Jeanie lifted the mug to her lips and sniffed. It smelt like hot tea, just as had been promised. She took a small sip and felt it slide down. It stroked a spreading warmth into the rigid metal plate of her run-hard stomach.

'Thank you,' she said.

She stood there amongst the goldfish crowd and drank the tea. She drank on, right down to the bottom of the mug.

Beneath the Coat Pile

A GUST OF wind pushed her into the café with a whoosh of her camel-coloured overcoat. The door clattered to behind her. She hesitated just inside the door, looking around. I could see the rain beaded on the tops of her feet where it had splashed onto her black high-heeled boots. I didn't recognise her, and she didn't recognise me. Not that either of us would have expected to.

I suppose it was obvious it was me. The only man sitting alone in the faded elegance of Nardini's Café. I'd been there a while, hypnotising myself by counting the waves breaking onto the promenade, riding them, watching for the seventh one—the big one. High winds are funny when you're right on the sea-shore because there's no reference point, no trees bending or loose signs creaking and batting the air. There's just the grey waves lumping in, a greyness stretching back to blend with the sky so it's hard to tell which is sea, which weather.

The bang of the door had left the latch unclosed, left it slightly ajar, so the draught sucked and blew across the ankles of the other coffee drinkers. It halted the empire biscuits just short of the mouths of the two women at the next table. They looked up with matching frowns, one framed by a brunette centre-parting, the other under a wavy white perm. They were obviously mother and daughter.

She approached my table. I rose slightly, not wanting to move too suddenly, to intimidate. I held out my hand to her.

'I'm Mike,' I said. 'Have a seat.'

She slid the camel coat off and sat down opposite me. Something invisible rustled beneath the surface of her clothes, some womanly secret of undergarments. Her mouth was red-varnished, her hair cut into a tight blonde bonnet.

'Have a coffee,' I said. 'Or an ice cream. It's what you're supposed to do here, isn't it? Though maybe not in winter.'

'Sorry I'm late.' She pulled the plastic menu towards her but ignored it, her gaze attaching to something high on the ceiling, the crystal cut waterfall of the light fitting. 'I haven't been in here for years.'

'My first time,' I said. 'Quite a place, eh?'

'I know what I'll have,' she said, wriggling slightly in her seat so that her clothes murmured again. 'I'll have the both together—ice cream *and* coffee. It's called *Affo*-something if I remember rightly. That's it—*Affogato*.' She stabbed a finger at the menu.

I motioned to the girl in the pinny on the other side of the room to take our order. When she'd finished writing and turned her back on us, the expectation began to prickle at me.

'Maybe she'll dance the drinks over to us,' I said. 'A quickstep or something. All part of the service.'

When she laughed, her teeth showed between the polished lips. And behind them, a deep red void blinked at me.

She pushed the menu to one side, clearing the way for some sort of business we had to deal with. After all, we were strangers really, just playing at familiarity.

'So,' she said, looking straight at me briefly and then turning away with a half snigger. 'So. Here we are.'

'Eight years later,' I said.

The coffees were brought over on flat, laced-up shoes, planted heavy on the sprung floorboards. The waitress didn't even step in time with the schmaltz that tinkled around the high ceiling, recalling an earlier time when it had cajoled dancers onto their feet. I sprinkled sugar into my cup. She dipped her teaspoon into the cream floating in hers. It was time then. I knew I had to start.

'So. Do you live nearby? In Largs?' I asked.

'Quite close. And you? Was it Edinburgh you said on the phone?'

I nodded. 'I moved away from Glasgow, not long after we . . . after the party.'

She looked into her *Affogato*. The firm edges of the ice

cream balls were already dissolving into the black coffee, spreading a brown cream across the surface of the glass.

'I'm not really in touch with Ken anymore,' I continued. 'With moving away and that. We didn't really keep in touch. What about you? Do you still see him?'

'Ken?' A line formed at the top of her nose. Specks of face powder and a few beads of moisture glinted briefly under the lamps. A doubt fluttered through me. Could this just be some nutter I'd accidentally lured in, not the right person at all? I hadn't thought about it all being a waste of time when I'd booked the day off work to get myself down here.

'The guy that had the party. You know? Ken.'

'Oh. "The Party".' The way she said it reassured me. 'No. Never did know him. I just tagged along with someone else, gate-crashing, as you do. Or did.' There was a slight twitch in her shoulders as she brought the glass up to her lips. When she put it down again, I could see a red stain on the rim. Did the lipstick not make the coffee taste funny, I wondered?

'What made you think of Largs?' she looked at me from under the fold of fringe.

'Sorry?'

'You put the ad. in the local rag here. How did you know I was living in Largs, then?'

'I drew a circle around Glasgow. Largs, Stirling, Dunfermline, Lanark. And so on.'

'And you advertised in all of them?'

'Yep.' I didn't tell her how long it took me to word the advert. So as to make the event unmistakable, but so as not to make myself sound like a complete weirdo. *Coat-pile monster seeks re-acquaintance with shocked girl in fish net stockings. Caird Drive party 1994.*

'Why?'

'I must admit, I was amazed when you replied. I'd been trying for ages. It was a long time ago now.' I watched my hands fraying the edge of the serviette. There was a block in my chest. Clearing my throat didn't shift it. I peeked up at her. She was still looking, her unanswered question prodding at me, her smile fixed. 'It's hard to explain,' I started. 'Sounds stupid. I just wondered . . . well, what happened next to you. I always just wanted to check. That you were OK.'

Afterwards, directly afterwards, I'd searched the rooms of the flat in which a party seemed to be in full swing whilst I was still smothered by a kind of sleep. I was deaf, my ears deadened by that sound, wincing as if eight outstretched fingernails were shrieking on a blackboard. With only the recollection of the fish-net feet and the dark-red oval, I set out to find her.

One room was packed with people, their limbs pounding through a mist of smoke and low light. They were apparently dancing with no music, to a beat I could only feel through the vibrating floorboards. In the kitchen, bottles smashed noiselessly onto the floor-tiles and faces bubbled up in front of me, smiling and speaking. I ignored them all, once I'd checked out their feet. I was on the other side of a glass wall, moving on in my sleep-search.

I even went back to Ken's bedroom to make sure I hadn't simply chased her around in a circle. The bed was half-lit from the small window above the door. It was a mess. A monstrous pile of coats coiled in a whirlpool as if something was about to spring from it. I even delved a bit under the coats, to make sure she wasn't under there. No one was there.

Then I searched the rooms in reverse order, looking for shoes. Could she have run straight from the flat, shoeless? I knew it was lashing rain, oozing puddles outside, and I imagined the fish-net stockings frayed and laddered. I saw her feet tripping in Partick potholes, splashed, lacerated. That was all there had been to know her by, in the semi-dark of the bedroom. Just her feet. Even the mouth I might just have imagined.

Outside, a weak sun parted the clouds and glittered on the breaking waves. The spray glistened white on the promenade, then turned black again. A light turning off.

'Why would it matter?' she asked. I looked at her and noted the slight ticking at the corner of her eye. As she recalled me to the café, to Largs, the table we were sharing, I became aware for the first time of her perfume projecting at me, heat-haze thick.

'Sorry?'

'Why would it matter what happened next. Whether I was OK or not?' She brought a serviette over her mouth and seemed to bite it. When she took it away, I noticed a bare area on her lower lip. The lipstick had been smudged, blotted onto her chin, almost as if she was melting. There was a slight shudder in the hair against her cheek. 'Why would it even matter what the hell I thought you were doing?'

'Believe me,' I said, 'I was intending to help.'

'Help?'

'Yes. You were upset. I could hear you. You were crying. After he'd gone, that bully—the guy you were with.'

'Do you know something, Mike?' She leaned towards me over the table. The lapel of her red jacket licked at the melted ice cream on the edge of her glass. 'Do you know, I'd actually forgotten I was even with a guy. I remember very little about that night.' She raised a finger and paused. 'Except for one thing. Except for you.' She flung herself back against the seat, arms folded. 'An honour, eh?'

'I'm not exactly flattered. I mean, I'm not exactly pleased with myself.'

She leant forward and pulled a small black handbag onto her lap and opened it. I wondered what she was going to show me. But then her head was twitching and turning, seeking the attention of the waitress above my head. A £10 note was pinched between red nails.

'I'll get it.' I fumbled for the wallet in my pocket. 'But don't go just yet. I really wanted to explain a bit more.'

She looked at her watch. But she didn't stand up.

'I just wanted to know if it changed anything. I really didn't mean to scare you. It was stupid. An accident. I'm honestly sorry. But I just wondered, with never seeing you after, I've been wondering for the last eight years. If it affected you? That's all.'

She laughed. The dark red void appeared again between the white cut of her teeth. 'Still the voyeur, then? Still peeking into other people's lives? Appearing in unwelcome places?'

'No. It wasn't like that.'

'Well, why did you do it then?' A silence clattered around us until it was broken by the scrape of chairs. The mother and daughter padded past our table on their way out. You could smell the disapproval. She watched them fasten the door catch, then flashed at me again. 'That's why *I'm* here. This isn't all about you, you know.' She was standing, pulling her overcoat off the seat. She had one arm in it already.

'Do what?' I honestly couldn't see what she was getting at.

'Hide. Spy on people. Jump out.' There was a ring of white all around her pupils. 'Well?'

I stood, fingertips on the tablecloth. The grey world

outside lashed at me through the window. 'I'd worked a double shift,' I said. 'This is what I wanted to explain to you. I went to Ken's early, to kip for a bit there before the party started. I lay down across the foot of the bed and laid my coat over me.'

'There was more than one coat,' she said. 'There was a bloody great pile of coats.' As she said it she pushed into the second arm of her own coat. She caught her hand on the back of the chair and glared at a broken nail.

'The other people arriving—they made me into a coat heap.' I tried to laugh. It was ridiculous after all. 'I didn't wake up. Not until I was buried. And roasting. When I looked out there were your feet, and his feet. There was some chat. A bit of an argument. Him leaving. You crying. Then I thought . . .'

'And you want to know if it changed me?'

'I thought I'd come out. Comfort you.'

'Like not going into dark rooms anymore. Ever,' she stared at me. 'Is that the sort of thing you meant?'

A jolt sat me down. I'd got a reaction.

'Yes,' I whispered.

'Like jumble sales being my worst nightmare—wondering what's under those heaps of clothes? Like seeing curtains transform into bodies, or ghouls or something? Is that what you wanted to know? You can make up the rest of the picture. Happy now?' She picked up her handbag. 'Now I've met you, I know you really are a

76

monster. You crawl out from under things don't you?'

She threw the £10 note onto the table and glanced across at the waitress. Then she flicked the coat into a wide arc and pushed out through the door. I saw the wind inflate her hair and pinch her eyes closed with the shock of exposure. She brought the two sides of her flapping coat under control, closed herself back in, and the black boots clip-clopped her out of sight along the esplanade.

When I followed her, I was caught for a moment in that same flattening of eyelashes against my face. I gulped at the air as the wind stole it from my nostrils. My eyes streamed. I ran towards the blur of her camel-coloured back. I hadn't even asked her name. I reached a hand out to her shoulder. And then she was sprung around and back from me, her scream crashing between my ears, forcing up my hands, beating down my eyelids. I heard that blast of fear, felt the air around me vibrate, glimpsed the mouth pulled back into a dark red oval void.

And despite my recoil, the grip and lash of that sound on me, my hand going up to pacify her, to make her see that wasn't what I meant. Despite all that, there was a small chink of something, like the clouds parting for a second to give a thrill of light. The recognition that had been lurking behind our conversation sprang out. It was fully formed now. I knew for sure. I had no doubt that she was the fish-net stockinged girl eight years on. I'd found her all right. And I'd unearthed the monster.

And the Sky was Full of Crows

THIS TIME AT least she could take the food right to him, rather than laying him a place across the table from her —the soup bowl, the mug, and the plate for a hunk of her home-made seeded bread—only to eat alone, trying to fill the empty space opposite with a jigsaw of remembered details. The leather watch strap he undid and fiddled with as he talked; the yellow spangles that sunlight sparked up in his brown eyes; the moss-green tweed with crossways of blue and purple.

'Bluebells and heather,' he'd said.

Even before, she would sometimes lay him a place to eat with her, as if sympathetic magic would draw him rustling to her cottage out of the woods and in the back door. Stealthy. Ever the stalker. Once he had surprised her as she stood at the kitchen sink. Out of silence his arms were suddenly tight around her; a growl in her ear. She'd swung around and slapped him hard across the face. A reflex.

'The big bad wolf, you are,' she'd said later, when they were both forgiven.

She had never known when he might be able to get away, to suspend the clock between the hill and his home. He always arrived hungry, grabbing with his peat-dark hands at lumps of bread to gnaw, cheese slabbed on top, a gulp of sweetened herb tea, which she had to stop him from putting milk in. And then her potter's fingers would reach out to his buttery lips, teasing the crumbs from the corners of his mouth.

She put on her warm, brown jacket. She had thought carefully about what to take him, what he would most appreciate. Into her cloth bag she put a plate she had made with the residents of the Centre, dimpled with their fingerprints, and a pottery goblet into which she would pour the Glenfiddich she'd found in the village shop. She'd seen how he loved the malts at the pub when his clients were paying. The only contact between the two of them then would be his sly wink.

She'd learnt that the blackberry and birch tree wines that she had poured from hand-corked bottles were not really his thing. After a while he had started to bring a bottle of Jacob's Creek or Blossom Hill from the shop, rustled to her cottage in a plastic bag. On summer evenings it had maddened her that they couldn't sit outside on the deck to drink it, because the other workers might see them, or the residents seek them out with their

79

adult-child curiosity and carnival faces.

'Midgies'll eat us down to the bone out there anyway, eh?' he'd say.

The field was soft as she walked across it, her feet soil-weighted in her wellies. A pheasant reared into the air out of long grass—a diagonal line of sleek russet feather trailing a clatter of shock. But she didn't take her eyes off the tall, still figure ahead, not until she knelt to lay each item on the ground in front of him.

She poured the whisky and put the prawn sandwich on the plate. No response. Just her own shiver, and the soft flap of the red overalls at the wrists, where the wind caught in them. It was like an invitation, the open arms. As if he was waiting for her body to press against his before he closed around her. But he wouldn't want that, not out here in the open.

He wore the red overalls for his farm work—when he was out helping his brother, gathering the sheep or mending fences—rather than the stalking. They were a kind of highland uniform. She saw them on men everywhere—riding quad bikes with collies crouched on the back, or in tractor cabs, or prodding bulls towards gateways with a stick. But she knew these overalls; she had found him.

He'd been wearing them their first time. Up there in the clearing, *her* clearing, the place she always went. In the long summer dusk they lay on their backs on the rug, heat-swaddled, bug-bitten, time marked by the crack and pop of the broom pods. Two empty wine goblets tumbled and lay next to them. They'd looked up through birch leaves and the sky was full of crows mustering and cawing amongst the tallest trees. And she had been the one who had rolled towards him, propelled with the sleepy desire of the sunshine and wine, her hand falling on the brass zip-tag of the red overalls, pulling it lower to put her fingers on skin and coarse hair.

Sometimes he drove the Landrover, full of hill-coloured clients, through the Centre. His window would be open, a flash of tweed cap, a tanned slab of cheek, a hint of the cute smile, and the moss-green arm with a hand rising half wave, half salute, turning into a loosely coiled thumbs-up to her before the Landrover lurched and crashed on the uneven track up into the hills. She would hear the guns all morning, the call of the beaters. She had jumped at each shot in the early days. But even the thud of the birds landing dead-weight in the bushes barely turned her head now.

When the Landrover returned at the end of the shoot, with its triumphant red-cheeked clients, he didn't turn his head to her, wary perhaps of her views. She'd been merciless when he put up the signs by the roadside: DRIVE CAREFULLY PHEASANTS.

'You're only going to shoot them, anyway. What does it matter to them *how* they die?'

81

And after that, when she drove towards their V-shapes tick-tocking across the road, stupidly slow, and they stopped mid-lane with their long, surprised, necks, she no longer swerved. She wasn't sentimental about death. Given the chance she would go to the back of the Landrover after a shoot to see the glossy sleeves of bodies lined up in the back, and later try to match in her sketch book the glamorous colours the sun had fired up in them.

'I'll be a potter in the next life,' he'd say. 'Won't need to breed or kill for my living then. Just get my hands dirty for art.'

It had been in her clearing that they'd first met. The sun was poking its fingers at her bare golden skin as she collected ideas for glazes into her sketch-book. It was the end of the day, when the colours were densest—gorse, spring bracken, a late greenish sky. She heard his laugh first, a ricochet of it. She had no idea how long he'd been standing there before she turned and saw him, a gun over his shoulder, the tweed jacket fracturing colour just as was intended, to camouflage him with the hill. Only his face. The sight of him should have triggered her prejudices against shooters, stalkers, country-types. But his boyish smile and his curiosity in her sketches arrested her before she fired a single insult.

'Come and see this,' he'd said.

She followed him to a place nearby, where they crouched low and silent, and watched five fox cubs basking with their mother in the late evening sun like kittens burnished by a fireside. There was no touch of hate or cynicism in his voice. 'The wee gingers,' he called them. And he didn't raise his gun, although the next time she went back, there was no sign of the family.

She made him a ceramic charm, a small eye. It wasn't so much to protect him, like the ones you saw in Turkey, the 'evil eye'. This one she made more human, with eyelashes and a bright blue iris painted onto it. He'd held it up next to her face.

'Like you,' he said.

'I'm keeping an eye on you'. She had dropped the clay coin into the breast pocket of his overalls, pulled the zip across.

∼

The food and drink lay untouched. The wind was inflating the red fabric and then beating it flat again. It wasn't in his character to be so silent and unresponsive.

'I'm just a wee boy trapped in a man's body,' he would say.

She stood in front of him. A faceless man. She opened her own arms wide to match his, closed her eyes and heard again the rough graze of his zip, the pop of the broom pods, rustle of the grass under them, and somewhere high above, the crows.

When the single shot had come that afternoon, she thought little of it, even though she knew it was out of season, hadn't seen a party bumping up the track in the Landrover. She'd got it from the gossip later, in the pub. Hushed voices and shaken heads. The fool, they said quietly, climbing a fence with his gun cocked, and with a wife and three children and all.

The crows kept their distance. They stayed high above the three identical, widely-spaced, red figures who protected the seeded ground. The only moving thing was the woman who had seemed to be dancing with one of them. She took something from the breast pocket, looked at it in her cupped hand and then hurled it, so it spun away from her across the autumn clay. She fell, became a small brown creature, crouched and barely visible on the mud. But her wail spilt along the ground, and coiled upwards to mingle with the crows' chorus in the big pale sky.

The Match

'WHY YOU TRAVEL alone?' the guy who runs the guest house asks. He sits down opposite me, as he has taken to doing after serving the evening meals, and up-ends the box of dominoes so that the pieces clatter across the table. I've told him several times already that I don't play. Sometimes I watch for a while as he gets a group of four together. I get hypnotised by the fast slam of pieces as excitement grows, the flicker of dark looks that cross the table diagonally, the curl of a lip that leads them all into laughter. It's hard to see why they find it so much fun. I usually get bored after a while and retreat from the veranda, go down the stairs and cross the night-cool sand to my cabin.

As he poses the question about me being alone, he rolls one of his dreadlocks between thumb and forefinger. The thick strands spring stiff and prickly above his forehead before separating over his neck and shoulders. They look like dark wool that's been felted by the weather, bleached at the ends. He presses and twiddles at it like a child might do with a lock of hair when they're watching TV or concentrating on something. His head's on one side, his tired eyes looking over my shoulder out towards the dark smash of waves. His domino pals haven't appeared tonight.

I shrug. I suppose I have to answer him, though of course I'm not going to tell him the real reason I'm alone.

'I'm just here to chill out,' I say, then hear my stupid words. The damp evening air wraps my shoulders like a heavy cardigan. I'm hardly going to get chilly here. 'I mean, relax. I'm here to relax. I don't need too much action.'

'You are relaxed now,' he says so that I can't tell if it's a question or a statement. He looks at me with a small grin, head cocked. 'You walk very fast when you first come.' He nods in the direction of the village and mimics scribbling with his hand. 'Very busy, writing postcards.'

I toy with one of the dominoes that landed in front of me. It's smooth and cool to the touch. I close my fingers around it. When I first arrived I stayed out of the public places—the veranda, the beach. I only went to the village to send Kenneth's postcards. I walked fast to rebuff the invitations that seemed to emanate from the groups of people under trees—heat-basking, laughing, working at unexplained things with their hands. Two men hunched over a big wooden board, played a game in which they shifted collections of tiny shells across a series of bowls carved into it. It was as if they were crouched with marbles or Pokémon cards in a school playground. But I only glimpsed them from the corner of my eye at first.

They don't hide their own fascination. The kids in the village run after me, want to stroke my straight blonde hair and pinch at my white skin. The way adults stop and study me isn't much different. I let my curiosity wander a little more too. He's right. I have relaxed.

'And tomorrow,' he says. 'Is your last day. Is a pity.'

I feel sick. Maybe a reaction. Something in the supper. Or something in the question, forcing me back to the gut-twisting mess Kenneth's made of our holiday together.

'Look at that, Kenneth,' I had pointed at a photo in the guide book. I was sitting next to him, grazing my fingers against the soft-coarse brush up the back of his head where the hairdresser had sheared him. In the photo, the sky-blue upper and turquoise lower were divided by a strip of white sand on which a *dhow* was landing. Its huge white sail cut a diagonal across the middle of the photo. It promised beauty and adventure and excitement. Kenneth squinted at the men in the water who were pushing the boat ashore, wearing straw hats and torn T-shirts.

'It looks kind of basic there.' A stray thought panicked his face out of the guide book. 'Will there be TV? There might not even be TV.'

'There'll be so much else to do, Kenneth, you won't

even miss it.' I laughed, nudging his reaction aside. After all, I had more or less persuaded him to go. I pictured us turning golden together, eating breakfasts of tropical fruit. Not being in a proper resort meant we wouldn't be hemmed in with other tourists. I'd have his undivided attention. He'd make me laugh like he did when we first met. Having a holiday together would cement things, make the future as clear as that turquoise water.

Lunch on my last day is kingfish and rice. As he lays the plate on the table in front of me, he flicks his head and scatters trails of hair, so they bounce soft against the skin of his face. It's like a mane. I can't help watching.

'What will you do for your last afternoon?' he asks.

'The usual, I guess.'

My curiosity strays in the sea breeze that blows though the upstairs veranda. Would it tickle or feel coarse—his hair? What would it be like to make love to someone with dreadlocks? Like the mating of lions—ferocious and soft at the same time?

I could tell Kenneth about this little fantasy when I get home. It might amuse him. I can almost hear him mutter, 'Larsson. Was it bloody Larsson you were dreaming of? Trust you to fraternise with the enemy. What are you playing at?' And I wonder how on Earth the picture of Larsson got into my head—the Celtic strip, and the swing of blond, Swedish dreadlocks. It's as if I've been brain-washed in my sleep.

I lie outside my cabin, in the shade, pouring along the hammock like an Arabian princess, belly rounded with rice and fish, toe trailing. All my books are finished and stacked up inside. I can occupy myself with indolence. Lying with the beach wind licking at my skin, I listen to the palm leaves rubbing and rustling against each other. Everyone else is resting after lunch. Dogs are dark flat shadows on the sand. There's a flash of reflected sun from way down the low-tide bleached runway of the beach, away from the safety of palm shade. A bicycle passing, sizzling in the heat on the white hard sand. Someone with an urgent crayfish delivery to a hotel, perhaps.

I buy a young coconut from the boy who comes each day with a bulging canvas bag. He slices a small lid off the top of the coconut and watches for a while, sitting in the sand as I drink the cool water from it. Afterwards he takes it back from me, slices the hole bigger with his huge grey knife and fashions a spoon from the spare husk. I know now what I'm supposed to do with it. I scoop out the soft white young flesh inside and let it slide sweet down my throat, barely chewing.

The boy huddles over three papayas and the glossy conch shell his mother has sent him out with. He shakes his head over them and every so often looks up at me. There aren't many other tourists here to sell things to. I've seen him in the evenings at the village playing field, freed from his marketing duties, running and leaping barefoot with the other boys, all straining to make contact with a bundle of cloth tied into a ball with string. And if I close my eyes, it could be the kids on the green at home. The cries collide with each other and ring with the same urgency and outrage and joy. The punch and bounce of a proper ball are missing, but the language is universal.

In the days before I left home, a white sheet of snow came down onto the green. It wrapped streets and cars and buildings. An easterly wind was spraying it into drifts as I pored over the small print of the travel insurance, and news came in that our ice maidens over in Canada had struck gold.

'The housework Olympics,' Kenneth said to my TV. 'All that sweeping up. Scotland's females excel at that, eh?' He peered at the hawk's hood of concentration on Rhona Martin's face as she sent the flat stone scudding across the ice. 'They look like plumbers' wives,' he said and turned to another channel.

Despite their victory, the girls still got pushed from the sports pages by pictures of footballers' muddy thighs. Somehow their ordinary names couldn't compete with the ones Kenneth recites, like Amuruso, Caniggia, Lovenkrands. I've never listened, but their names have taken hold somehow. They make me think of exotic desserts, full of cream and liqueur.

'You can't change the dates,' I told Kenneth. 'Death, illness, injury, bereavement, redundancy or jury service. We'll just have to lose the booking money. Or go.'

The heat's bearable now as I meander barefoot back on the firm shore, out in the open where the breeze fans and cools me. I haven't been all the way to the village. There's no point in sending postcards now, and anyway I've stopped thinking of things to tell him.

Because it's the east coast, the wind-lain palm trees are shading the beach, the squat, thatched houses hiding between them. The trunks of a few trees standing alone are filament-thin, cut by sunlight from behind. One of them, a crazy hieroglyphic, is a signpost for me. The trunk of the twisted palm outside my guest house.

I see the figure on the beach from quite a distance. As I close in, I can see that he is naked except for shorts—the uniform of late afternoon recreation. For men, anyway. The figure is dancing on the spot. The feet point down, knees rise towards the chest one at a time, arms wing-like at the sides. It's balletic. It's as if the figure's on a vertical spring, bouncing rhythmically, perfectly balanced. But it's not until I'm quite close that I see the ball that's part of the dance too. He rolls it back and forwards on the sand, under each foot, then hooks a toe under it to flick it into the air. It rebounds from a raised knee; the chest pushes out to butt at it; the figure pirouettes to catch the bounce against his lower back.

The features refine as I get nearer the twisted palm. A bump of something on top of the head—dreadlocks tied into a knot, their ends flopping onto the back of the neck. The rounded muscle on arm and thigh and chest. Full lips, dark eyes, nostrils flared in concentration.

'Why do you play alone?' I ask when I get close enough for him to notice me.

He stops the ball in his hands and shrugs.

'You can play too,' he says, and drops the ball onto the ground.

'No, no, I can't. I don't.' I turn for my cabin.

'Is easy. Look.' He kicks the ball towards me. 'You're the goal first, then me.'

I don't understand. How can I be a goal?

'Like this.' He stands with his feet wide apart. 'I'm the goal. You shoot.'

The ball has rolled to a stop in front of me, hard to ignore, teasing me to attack it. With his feet apart he seems to have dropped in height, so we are eye to eye. He nods. I take a step back and gather my breath and concentration, my bare foot and poor vulnerable toes. I kick it, straight between his feet. Clean. A clear-cut goal. A rush of something bounds me up and down.

'I've never done that before.'

'Now my turn,' he says. 'The first one to three goals is the winner. If I win, you have to make a presentation to me. If you win, I make to you. OK?'

'Present what?'

'The presenter chooses.'

'OK,' I hesitate while I mentally rifle my luggage for something I don't need which would make a suitable gift. The first thing I think of is a comb, a nice turquoise one. Then I look at his head and remember. Of course, he doesn't use a comb.

He dribbles the ball along the beach, the knot of his hair bouncing. I grin, but his eyes grip the space between my feet. He kicks hard and the ball bumps my foot, bounces away from the goal. I grab it.

'My turn,' I say, scenting victory. I picture myself holding the shiny cup handles, the roar of the stadium pushing the trophy up above my head. Would Kenneth believe that I actually *played* football? And enjoyed it.

'But what will you do?' Kenneth had glared at me when I said I'd go on my own. I only said it to get a reaction. I really couldn't imagine what anyone would do on holiday on their own. But it might just make him change his mind if I called his bluff.

'I mean,' he'd said. 'You're not really going to find a table-tennis club in a place like that. Are you?'

'I'll take a pile of books. I'm not a child you know—I don't need games. I just need a holiday.' Saying it almost made me believe it.

'But you're hardly a lone ranger, pal.'

'Come with me then.'

He tipped his head on the one side, creased his eyes like he was dead sad about it. 'You know I can't, love.' He took my hands, swallowed hard like he was going to tell me someone had died or something. 'I know you're not a big fan of the game. It's hard for you to understand, but . . . You do know this match could mean the quarter finals, don't you?'

Those turquoise waters froze into a lump in my throat. And then I knew I'd have to see the bluff through. I went upstairs right then and opened a suitcase on the bedroom floor. I dropped things into it as I thought of them, when I passed it over the next few days.

When I left my flat for the airport, I noticed the black tarmac rectangle that Kenneth's car had cut into the snow, where he'd been parked. His car had been there a lot in recent weeks. And now it was marking out his territory even when he wasn't there. But then, it was starting to snow again.

I look at my watch by the candlelight that the wind flickers across the supper table, and calculate the hours across the oceans. The match will be about to start now. Somehow I know the kick-off time. How sad. The pub will be bubbling with testosterone, wall to wall with blue nylon, Kenneth at the centre of it. They'll be gripping pints at the bar, repeating the ritual stories, 'Mind that time when Beanie. . .?' And after the laughter's bent them double, they'll practise the usual jokes. There's the one about not swerving to hit a cyclist who's a Celtic fan. Because it's probably your bicycle. And something about Celtic fans and dole queues. I'm always careful not to take the bait, but I suspect he laughs a lot louder when I'm not about.

After the evening meals have finished, and the other diners have left the veranda for their cabins, he beckons me to join him behind the bar. He gives me a stool to sit on. This is new. Not joining me at the table. No dominoes. The breeze from the night sea has swelled up so much that my skin almost puckers into goose bumps. He pours a glass of something creamy coloured.

'What is it?' I ask.

He pushes the bottle towards me and points at the label. I have to peer closely because it's gloomy behind the bar. There's an elephant and some round yellow fruit.

'This tree, wild marula. They call it the "elephant tree".' He puts the glass in front of me. 'This is your prize. For winning the football match.'

'Thank you. A grand prize,' I say, still glowing from my victory.

He lays a hand over mine as I reach to take the glass.

'But there's a special way to drink it. A game.' He picks up the glass, its contents luminous pale against his small, pointed fingers. 'You take a drink, then pass it to me.'

It takes me a moment to get what he means, to realise that I somehow already know the rules of this game. I open my mouth for him. He pours sweet cream onto my tongue and I hold it there while eye burns on eye and his teeth glint in a soft smirk, waiting. I circle the drink in my mouth. It tastes smooth and strokes the bare skin of my neck and arms back to warmth. Then I'm slipping towards him from my stool, and pouring from my mouth into his, slippery with fruit and cream, drinking.

We are the same height. Knee to knee, chin to chin, each limb fits the other. I feel the graze of tendrils sprinkling against my face. His hand silks at my hair.

No one's watching. Eyes at home will be fixed on a Dutch stadium. I'm part of the game now, as a player, not a spectator. My hands are on the back of his head, closing soft on dreadlocks, stroking his mane.

Kiss of Life

FOUR KISSES GOT me here. A pocketful of kisses. A plague of them.

The first was an exploration—probing new places with tangling tongues. A tightrope of saliva glinted in the sun as we stretched apart. It was maybe where I got it, what my mother calls the 'kissing disease' and the doctor called glandular fever. I don't care about the name, just that I've spent the last month swimming through treacle.

Then Mum's kiss on my cheek, dispatching me to recover at Anne and Bill's hotel. Sending me far away from my discoveries with Simon. She's a good girl, I heard her say on the phone. She'll be no bother, I promise.

The third, you could describe as a kiss. Lips meeting red-ripe skin, teeth piercing, juice bursting on my tongue. The back of my hand wiping away sugar crystals and fluorescent stains. Strawberries, kissed under the evening sky, leaving seeds to swell dark inside me.

And of course the one I refuse. Watching her body heavy and motionless in the sun, keeping my distance, spellbound by the white legs straight and still. She was waiting for a kiss I didn't want to give; a kiss that would be red and blue and icy as the mountain stream.

Too busy with meals and rooms, Anne gives me a pink-jacketed map. Walking's the pathway back to health, she says. I try to please, following dotted lines on the map in spider's legs from the hotel as each day circulates with no clear beginning or end. I feel the weight of mountains towering above me. The spaces between things are so big; there are so few houses, not a single shop. I never seem to get far before my legs waver, and I need the shelter of my bedroom again. I return with hanging limbs to let my body doze while my mind clambers onto some kind of roundabout. I've got used to it these days—the thoughts that unravel in slow motion in a curtained room. Each one turns on an unoiled cog, labouring its way through a backwards logic, being overtaken by the next.

I pull the curtains across my window but they don't meet in the middle. Or if I make them, they leave a gap at the side, a vertical slot through which dark forests, mountains, and daylight glare in at me. The world outside won't quite leave me alone. My hotel room should be a sanctuary but it's not peaceful. A faint scratching shudders against the walls, and the shrieks of something soaring in the sky outside pierce walls, doors, windows. I peer upwards through the slot in the curtains and trace the shrieks to the arrow-shaped birds which swoop and flicker in circles, greedy for midges and flying ants. They chase each other in arcs into the eaves above my window.

They're swifts, Bill told me. They can't land on the ground you know.

I hear them late at night, long after birds should be in their nests, whistling so high over the night air. I imagine them circling and shrieking all through the night, never resting, till presumably they die of exhaustion, in flight.

Anne bustles in and out of the breakfast room, a glimmer of familiarity amongst silver teapots, deers' heads on the wall, porridge on the menu, different guests every day. Toast—that's all I want. I push away the bowl of jam. A wasp settles in it, legs scrabbling in the red. It's in wasp heaven, feasting stickily, until it becomes too entangled in its own pleasure. Stuck. In too deep to escape.

You must eat a bit more, Anne says. You're here to get strong. I can't let your mum down. By the end of the week you'll be running as strong as that river out there, you'll see. Anne bobs down to window level and points at the silver thread which cuts through the land. Even from here I'm dazzled by the sun colliding off the leaps and dashes of water through rocks as the river pursues its descent.

There's nothing wrong with me now. No sore throat

99

anymore, I say. I'm just tired; I need to sleep. But it doesn't seem to be that easy.

One morning early in the week the daylight wakes me, gets me out of bed, calls me to the window. I don't want to upset Anne by being late for breakfast. The usual view greets me—the hills backing the flat sheet of floodplain, the standing stone guarding the river, the phone box red at the end of the road. My watch says 4.30 a.m.—it's not breakfast time at all. But there's a day already underway out there, one we know nothing of, getting on without us while we sleep. At first I can't make out what makes it so still, but as I watch I realise it's because there are no people. I feel like an intruder into a world I'm not supposed to see, like a child peering from the stair landing onto an adult party, trying to fathom the laughter which swells and skips between guests with no apparent reason.

I'm ready to retreat but with a lurch I realise my mistake. There *is* someone, standing by the phone box. She's so still I hadn't noticed her. A girl with long orange hair who stares up at me. The swifts swoop over her, greedy for the air around her head, daring to sweep closer and closer. Her only movement is the chewing of her mouth at something as she stares. I snap the connection of our gaze, pull back the curtain, and return to bed, protecting myself from the eyes of this other day, trying to dispose of the image of the girl. Maybe I just imagined her. In this daylight night anything seems possible.

I continue to explore the local area; the strength in my legs dictating how far I go. In the field opposite the hotel, I skirt around a grassy mound left ragged and wild amongst the cultivation. THE MOUND OF THE DEAD, a sign tells me. Bodies were brought here after the plague in the fourteenth century; pulled by an old lady with a white horse. How would it be to die of the plague—did they catch it from kissing too? Did they waste away, not wanting to eat, walking shorter distances each day? Did the bony fingers of midsummer prod their eyelids open, not allowing them to rest? I imagine, under the thin soil of the mound, a pit holding the tight embraces of arms and legs, necks coupling, heads buried under the weight of limbs, fingers caught in one another's hair. I feel the press of Simon's arms around my ribs and back, his weight on me, heat passing from skin to skin. But their embraces would be cold and clammy, and the weight of so many bodies too much to bear.

A faint path entices me towards the river to catch the shade under the trees. In the next field the bent backs of berry-pickers are pressed down by the sun. I've seen their produce in plastic tubs at the end of the track, the red letters on a white board signalling STRAWBERRIES, RASP-BERRIES. They're sold to passing tourists with pots of cream, and to locals for making jam. Maybe to spread on toast, maybe just to trap the wasps.

In the gaps between trees, white light sparks off the

river as it spills over rocks. It stabs at my eyes, punctuating the leafy gloom. Tree shade, river light, tree shade, too bright. Mesmerised by the strobe show, I feel sick.

Then, through the trees, above the crackling of water on rocks, a scream rushes at me, stops the pulse of my steps. Through trembling leaves I see snatches of arm, leg, shoulder. A group of women and girls are in the river, their jackets and skirts thrown off to expose skin to sun and water. They must be taking time away from the berry fields. Laughter follows the scream. They are ankle deep in the water, just off a shingle bank. The girl with orange hair is there too. She stands deeper than the others, green dress tucked into her knickers, her thighs ash-white. She scoops the river into her hands, throws it at the paddlers. Her laughter sweeps and swoops around the group, tumbles through her loose hair with the sunlight. She falls backwards, letting the river close over her head, then springs back to her feet with snorts of water and laughter. I guess she's my sort of age, shrieking with life, so unlike the motionless figure she was the other night. I retreat into the shadows before the women should see me, before the effort of speech.

The scene reminds me of lying on a riverbank with Simon, a wider river than this, without rocks. A friendly sun, tickling grass, the crawl and nip of ants across bare legs, the whisper of his eyelashes against my cheek. There was a smell of something, like a kind of pollen, but it makes me think of garden plants in the street at home, not the wild sort you get here. We turned to devour each other in the moments between passing pleasure boats. I wiped away our mingled saliva with the back of my hand.

Simon, so far away. Missing him. You'll meet people there, Mum had said. Maybe there'll be folk your own age in the village you can get friendly with. I don't think so Mum. There's just a gap where Simon was. His kisses sent a tickle into parts of me quite distant from my mouth. A tickle I want more of. Was I getting in too deep, like the wasp stuck in its own jam feast?

We never went in the water like the berry pickers. Even though I love to swim, I'm a strong swimmer, have a life-saving certificate. Simon said there might be things in the water—bacteria or bugs, and it was dangerous anyway, almost as if he was afraid. Perhaps the river here is a different beast, cleaner water straight from the mountains, with more shallows and pools to protect the heat-dazed. I'm not sure though. I have a feeling it's just disguising its anger, acting demure as it seeps slow through the flood-plain. I've seen the dark ravine it tumbles out of just a little upstream—a torrent that could catch you up, entangle you in its tendrils of current, seizing the muscles in your arms and legs.

Later, I find the orange-haired girl standing by the phone box when I want to talk to Simon. It's as if she's waiting for the phone, but no one's using it. She stares at me, unsmiling, winding her hair around one hand. She has wide lips, fattened further by a red stain. Her eyes stay on me though the glass.

As I come out of the phone box, she holds out to me strawberries in a plastic tub. With the other hand she feeds herself one, its brightness blending with her own vivid mouth. I think of her unwashed hands all over the strawberries, her sneezes even. But I take one because I don't want to seem unfriendly. I'm close enough to her now to see a strawberry seed dried onto her chin. She pulls a paper bag from her dress pocket and holds it open. Sugar. She nods my hand into the bag. It clothes the strawberry in a gritty white coat which crackles on my lips as I bite in. Juice squirts into my mouth. The craft of the strawberry. It coils around my tongue with its sweetness so that I can't think for a moment. Boss-eyed. Drugged. She watches me. It's as if she's watching me in the intimacy of a kiss.

Thanks.

She sits down on the ground, back to the wall, hunches over cigarette papers and tobacco, rubbing something into the open paper, concentrating.

Where do you stay? I ask, trying to like her.

She points a red-stained finger across the field to the cluster of vans and trailers beyond the mound of the dead, near the river. People are standing in the open doorways, sitting on warm evening steps amongst children and bicycles.

Tinks, Bill had said. They come for the berry picking every year. Always have done. Always will, I guess.

I wonder if they are the plague survivors.

She doesn't withdraw the cigarette when I tell her I don't smoke. It's long and lumpy; not like one from a packet. I take a puff. I already know I don't like it. And anyway I'm a good girl. Another puff so she won't think me dull, then I give it back. Shiver. Crumpling legs. I sit down next to her. Everything drifts sideways, going blank like it does for the Hollywood spy whose drink has been spiked. A chain of her words process past me. First their meaning, then their tune fades until I just watch the red lips chewing them out. She mouths a story that seems to hold me down for hours, a day, a night. I hear nothing. All I know is that I must get back to my room. I claw myself back towards her words, grasp at the moment, push the nausea down. She blows smoke, thrusts more strawberries at me.

Eat one. Sweet.

No. I have to go.

I stagger to my feet, propelled by the need to stretch a distance between us. I feel her eyes pursue me as I focus hard on the line to the hotel. The image of her red mouth works on in my mind until I seal her out with the door.

On my back, the curtains gape at me. My ears close down, heart thudding into them. Amplified in my right ear, something nibbles, scratches, crunches. It doesn't stop when I move my leaden head. I search the shell of the room from the bed and then pull myself upright to circle it with probing fingers. I find a wasp, mauling at bare wood on the doorframe. Its front legs act as a brace, as it pumps its mouth back and forward against the wood, gnawing a furrow. It's so loud for so small a thing. But when I fall back on the bed, the nibbling noise continues in my ear, burrowing its way through my brain, drowning in the sticky jam of my thoughts.

As I fall towards sleep, the room fills with water and I slide into the cold gasp of it from the edge of my bed, letting it hold me, seep into me, filling up the empty parts of me.

I don't walk the next day. I avoid the phone box, abandon Simon to be free of her shadow, stay in my room. My throat feels constricted, my face prickles.

I hear Anne on the phone to my mother: A bit of a relapse today, I think. I can't get her to eat much. No, no bother at all, she says. Very quiet.

And I want to ask, how long can one week be?

Anne brings me a bowl of strawberries at lunchtime. Sweet. So sweet. Eat.

But I don't trust them. They turned my night upside

KISS OF LIFE

down. Or was it the sugar, the cigarette, something else she did to me, the orange-haired girl? She made this chaos emerge out of me like a creature that's hatched from an egg, and is now finding its wings.

That night I see her again, at ease in the other day, the daynight. She bends over something, near the standing stone. I try to stretch the curtains across her but the image remains, burnt into my eye. The glint of orange hair, and the shock of the red-stained mouth, even from a distance.

Then something starts to eat away in my imagination. Lying on my bed, I picture her ill in her caravan, unable to work in the berry fields, tossing and restless, trickling tears. She wouldn't trouble me then. I let the idea grow. She becomes a plague victim; dress tucked into knickers, her limbs matching white with the horse who drags her to the pit. Something unfastens in my throat, loosens its grip. A flourish of energy seeps through my body. It's quieter than the energy I had before I was ill, moving in unfamiliar currents. As I lie behind the protection of curtains, I feel the charm begin to work—my visualisations creeping into life, becoming possible. I become stronger and she more feeble. It raises a smirk behind my hand. I allow my imagination to delve deeper. How many other ways might there be to stifle her hold on me?

You're lucky, Anne insists. This is our heat-wave. Take a book to the river. Some strawberries maybe.

Blasted with sunlight, the mountains vibrate behind the floodplain haze of river, the mound of the dead, the backs bent in the berry fields. The orange hair isn't visible, not yet. I drop my blanket, my book. I'll stop here, stay well away from the pickers. I plunge onto the blanket, into a pool of heat and shade. I half read, half sleep, in a shimmer of leaves and grass, until footsteps jar the ground under my ear, urgent and fast.

A child bursts through the trees near me, runs toward the pickers. He stumbles, head turned over his shoulder, slaps chest to thigh into the man picking in the first raspberry row. The man straightens, listens. His bellow shakes the air, jolts the surrounding mountains. He runs towards me, his mouth transforming into a square hole as he gets closer, the rasps of breath louder, and then louder. He turns before he reaches me, splashes into the river, pulls something onto the bank. A mound with a green sodden dress, orange hair saturated black, white legs straight and still. Up from my blanket, I creep closer. Sunbathing on the bank, her face looms at me, blue with red-stained lips. In too deep. She was in way too deep.

The man kisses at her lips, raises his head to shout, tries again. He looks up at me, his face swimming.

You do it. Do you know how?

I shake my head. I don't want to kiss her taste of strawberries, sugar, and her mountain-cold breathless mouth. I shake my head and watch him kiss and blow. His eyes plead up at the gathering faces. He strives for her life but doesn't tip her head back far enough to clear the windpipe.

The berry field empties people onto the river bank. The air fills with screams and sobs. Someone runs to the phone box. I sink down, crouch in the grass, watching. They hold her body, turn her over. Her hair and dress come alive with stolen river water, streaming. But the limbs remain stagnant. I imagine the paper bag, soggy in her pocket, the sugar crystals dissolved, their mischief diluted, mingling sweet with the river water as it twists away downstream.

The ambulance siren and the sobs ebb away, leaving me alone in the field as the day softens to dusk. I lie on my back on the mound of the dead, my arms and legs seeping into the shared bed. The hills and sky lurch over me in a protective arch. Swifts shriek, scooping the air inches from my head. My hand strays into a pocket. I place a strawberry against my lips and kiss its flesh entirely away from the spidery stalk. Sweet. So sweet. The best sort of kiss.

The Weight of the Earth and the Lightness of the Human Heart

THERE'S A BODY on the hill. It's not dead yet, but lying very still. I might have taken it for a victim of your cold blast, your deathly grasp. But on the eve of Beltane, your powers are sunk too low to squeeze with your bony fingers at a human neck. Now the body's on so obscure a heathery ledge that your ice-sharp eyes won't pick at it, not without my help. Even the herons that creak along behind you will miss it in this smear of fog and night.

There's something strange about its position, one arm splayed awkwardly above its head. The man refuses to move, even to curl himself into the plastic survival bag he has carried for half a lifetime. At the bottom of his ruck-sack, the bag is rolled against a sediment of oat cake crumbs. Their gradations enumerate his hill walking years —last season's gravel rattles amongst earlier deposits, now ground to a fine sand. But he refuses to move. And so the rucksack pushes up his shoulder blades, thrusting his chest in a barrel to the sky, increasing the elegant curve of that arm that sinks back into the dripping moss. He seems to await the end.

I watched his progress—how the body was slowed to fumbling by lack of food, and the whisky that burned from flask to empty belly. How he slipped on the rocks of the ridge and allowed himself to slither and then pitch, thwacking rocks on the descent. Perhaps you heard, whilst wheeling this season's last circles on the wings of my winds? The weight carried him down with no resistance. He fell like the massive exhalation of a sigh, perhaps with a grain of surprise at the power with which the Earth pulled him down to it, reclaiming him. 'Take me, then,' he said, and fell, easily, to obscurity.

The man remains inside the body, but he teeters between clinging on and escape. He sinks into the bog, its dark juices oozing around him. Each groan releases him deeper under the mantle of night. He is slipping into oblivion.

Shriek with your dying laughter if you must, but if we took a hammer and chisel to this man, you might understand the weight of human cares. We would reveal the hidden landscape, the hardness which dictates his crust. Come look, put down your staff. Chip down through the strata of sadnesses and see here, in this black seam, as if laid down by a melting glacier, the friend recently buried by liver cancer. There's the soft-eared terrier, his walking companion, crushed under a Salvesen truck. Go deeper and find the lover left behind in Turkey when he was a young man; the father who died in his second year. This layering of pains, these strata, are what make up the man. Like the Earth, he is created from the inside.

Notice now (come closer, you're not so weak yet) how this final addition, like the topmost weighty stone placed carelessly on a cairn, threatens to topple the order of the rest. Bearable pains cease to be so. His sadnesses, which have seemed individual, some not even realised, now connect underground like mycelium, fastening together into a cloak which wraps the man, not warming him, but immobilising his limbs and paralysing his heart. This is what has brought the man here, for you to claim if you will, in your last glacial gasp.

And this one addition to his pains? The woman, Marion, has gone from him.

Strange, how he allows the memory of a smell to haunt him. I followed him back through the years to discover something she sprayed to glisten her arms. The fresh scent trailed after her, wafted by her hands, and he was mesmerised by the bittersweet astringency. It reminded him of hippy oils that coiled around the rooms of adolescent parties. I've seen men intoxicated, numbed by your rimey strokes till they speak slurred nonsense. But this was a human enchantment.

'It's just moisturiser,' she told him. 'But it keeps midgies away too. Those boys use it, working on the Skye bridge, with the hard hats and beefy biceps. Nancies, eh?' But far from repelling him, it drew him close. To him, this fractional, human rush of him to her, the miniature violence of their embraces, was a continental waltz. He felt the force of their collision, as one which thrusts the Earth into mountainous buckles and folds.

And now. It happens to all of them, once they've accumulated the rocks and boulders of the years. Like this man, they are pulled into the soil by the weight of pain. They reach a balance between life and a dwindling, seeping, letting go. They will return to the bog, a release with nothing but a small show of bubbles.

He wasn't like our normal hill walkers, the ones you crackle after, eyeing for opportunity. I saw how the keeper, who opened the gate for him at the start of the walk (to him, another world ago) looked at him with approval. He noted the corrugated boots, decent gear for the hill, the rucksack suggesting preparedness. He registered the knowing way the man orientated his map and compass. The keeper swatted at a black cloud of midgies around his head as he said, 'The buggers are here already, aye, so early in the season.' He gestured at the damp shroud submerging the tops, and told him how 'they're lurking up there too, waiting'.

As the cuckoo called behind them, the keeper watched

the man with the map. His finger crossed the lines which spread and angled and lay against each other to describe this rocky place. How foolish of them not to see the slim shard of time it represents. The lines on the map gesture towards past petrifactions, bubblings and foldings. But they give up no trace of the shifts and rifts to happen tomorrow.

Then the keeper saw the man put the map away in his pocket, slide the red arrows on his compass to lay one over the other, and march away on zero degrees, not even on the path.

I watched him, long after the keeper had turned away to his work on the estate. So you see, my bony-shouldered friend, it was as if I drew him on, sucking him towards me with my strong-muscled cheeks. The compass was back in his pocket, but he walked on, as if the orientation was hard-wired in his brain, like an arctic tern migrating north in summer, following the daylight to my realm.

He waded blaeberry and bog cotton, his boots clattering across your deep-clawed scratches on the limestone pavement. His head was bent to some human pilgrimage of despair that I was unable to interpret. Like the salmon, sniffing its way back up-river to its birthplace through the familiar sequence of reversed smells—pine-perfumed currents, granite flavoured ground-water, soft sediments—he seemed to discern his path. Do not ask me why he came so desperately towards me. No, it's not for me to know everything, not every small thing, my dear.

He noticed the puddles lying in moats around moss-lined rocks, and he saw, reflected in the sleek surface, the clouds that scudded across them. This was all the puddles gave him at the beginning. He climbed higher, into the mist, a black speck against white where he crossed the snow pockets still clutched jealously by the wrinkles of the hill, just as you cling to the months of ice. Then the reflection of the sky was lost to the bog pools, and he looked deeper.

It was faint at first to him, just the hinted arc of an eye-socket. He drank whisky from his flask and saw the dull embossed band across the forehead of one, and at the next, the faint shape of rusted shutters across the chest and over the shoulders, protecting the heart. This he knew to be exactly the defence he should have had. I saw him laugh at this thought, slow and stumbling, and his hands flapped at his open coat as if in an attempt to close himself against your parting gusts. A slight shiver shook at him.

Head to toe, caged foot to cased elbow, heads butted up against each other, he saw the brotherly warriors waiting under the bog. He saw that the metallic scales would still clink if they rose out of the bog and were shaken, like the terrier sprinkling water from its coat. He walked on with the certainty that the warriors slept with eyes peeled back and ears awaiting the signal to rise. As he looked darker, beyond reflections of the upper world, he recognised in an unblinking pupil, their deeply resigned waiting.

It seemed to me that the company brought a strange comfort to his journey.

He shouldered the hill there, ignoring the summit with its scattered decoration of teetering boulders, the conical thrust of it from the hot heart below. He found a route through the castellations sculpted by your frosty shatterings. He stretched up, hands numbly gripped on damp rock, clutching on the hanging honey-bells of heather, persuading his right foot onto a high step. And he was ambushed. Not by you my dear, let's not flatter your fading energy, but by his own mind.

He crushed a herb under his palm, close to his face. The smoky scent of bog myrtle caught at a memory, nudged his body out of balance, excavated a huge chasm of breath from him. I pursued his vision—I admit to curiosity in this human mystery. A younger Marion came smiling from a greenhouse into sunshine with a bowl of ripe tomatoes. Her hair fluttered, sweet with the juice of basil leaves she had brushed against. He circled her and the bowl in his arms, inhaling, drawn inevitably close. In mid-stride on this hill, his 20 years of life with her, a barely discernible grain of time, expanded and became (to him, my dear, to him) the heaviest boulder that all us gods could shoulder. The nudge of heat and smell, added to despair and stupor, was all he needed to topple. The rest you know.

Now he's finding his peace with the cold water flowing

through the thousand crumbled years of growth recorded in the peat. He sinks towards that rock from which he was chipped, back to where it came from, under the sea. Soon he'll lose his edges, merge back, like glaciers in an ice age. He feels the relief of it, no doubt.

He cannot move. Darkness hangs above him, moisture beading on the skin of his face, the face like a map of his past. Put a finger to that line and he could tell you its origin, the history of its formation. He won't tell you now, of course. But he would have done in the smoke-filled bar last night, as he uncoiled himself from his ten-hour drive. And perhaps that was the meaning behind the joke he made with the keeper, when he pointed to the lines of the map. 'Like my face,' he'd said, and the keeper had felt the too-long laugh of the man, like a splinter under his finger-nail, for the rest of the day.

Something's happening. This bang. It punctures our still mountain night, though the man barely observes it. He hears the signal that comes a second time. From beneath the bog, he knows it as the rallying call, mistakes it for the Fingalian horn, and awaits the third. Briefly, in the sky he sees the descent of a blurred globe of light. Briefly, it's clear enough to sparkle and then is reabsorbed into the damp thick air, a smudge borne back to the peat. He even hears the hounds. They suggest to him the clink and clank of old armour being shaken down. He imagines it resettling to the broad silhouettes of men as they rise upright, reinvigorating the gristle in their arms and legs, stretching and shaking, ready for their calling after so many centuries. The recognition of it all would have pulled a nod from him, if he could move. But he is fading from them, exchanging places with them, sinking. What does he care for the fight to which they are called, when he is slipping far away?

Now watch! Unblinking, his eyes take in, but do not grasp, the string of torch-light below. It coils and lengthens on the hillside, blurs through fog, scatters and reforms, fragments of it bitten black by the crags stepping between them. It would draw his eyes to the world below, to the valleys of human life that he deserted some hours before. But his eyes remain blank.

Hounds again, baying.

Deep voices echo, muffled in night drizzle.

Steps resonating in the bog, submerging to thud at the rock.

You can barely see the man now, so insignificant has he become with dark and cold and sorrow. Touch, if you will, his skin so pale and cold. But even with the prods of your bony fingers, he is now beyond the effort of shivering. The bog is closing around him, embalming. A solitary entombment.

Now is the time to gather your creaking strength. Despite the late hour, the grass growing fast beneath you, its sap draining you, he's yours, he's carrion. He's your last act of ice before you hurl down the staff.

You are too slow. Ah, but, my dear, your jealous screech lacks its winter command. It fails to penetrate the skies and peaks. But don't go yet, not on this sour note. Watch, how the torches snake towards him. See how the army, swift of foot, bulky and bearded, spread their light, huge burdens lumping their broad shoulders. Giants. Men of rock. See how they build themselves into a circular fortress, now they have found the body, and their search is over.

The largest kneels beside him, a flash of red in the torch-light. The fallen man, still just a fragment of him clinging inside the body, observes the tickle of something coarse on what used to be his face, and a breath of wind, hot and hoarse and regular. He hears the creak of stiff clothing, and feels warmth leach from something next to him. Strong arms wrap him in the mightiest of hugs, partially lifting him from the sucking bog. And in the deep breath he pulls in, curling with summer warmth, loaded with memory, comes that intoxicating scent.

Follow me. Look. How the memory of Marion whispers at the consciousness of the fallen man, as the bittersweet smell gushes within the survival bag. It is her smell. Her skin so soft. A whoosh of speed and light plummets the man deep back inside the body. A shock kicks with his heart. The sharp pain of his shoulder crashes in, as his heart pulses out to his limbs, to his grazed knees and gashed elbow. He takes deep breaths of Marion, opens his

119

eyes and looks straight into the brow-heavy eyes of the warrior, who smoothes his hand along the man's arm, gives up his warmth to him, tells him he is safe now, quite safe.

Take that chisel now and look closer, my dear. Come on, be kind for once, you have lost him anyway. Tap gently. You'll discover something between the black strata we saw earlier. A slight rearrangement perhaps, or just a different way of looking. His daughter expects her first child in this slim golden seam. And look here, the quartzite glint of his friend Mike who will take him to walk the Pyrenees next June. Here's the mother, silver-haired and framed, smiling comfort into the flat where his unpacked boxes are still scattered across the floor. In seeking his wilderness, he has stumbled upon an unexpected mine of treasures.

Dawn is promising its dewy light as the torches of the rescue team part and cross, midgies are swatted, a stretcher is constructed, flasks are cracked open, the alsatian is stroked and rewarded with biscuits.

The body on the hill leans without resistance into the offered embrace.

'Thank you,' he murmurs.

The red warrior cased in Goretex next to him, the man with the cradling arms and thick beard, clamps the man closer to him, turns aside his face, and from the fiery core of his human being launches a whoop of life. It reaches up high into the morning sky, lifted like floating bog cotton by the dawn's small birds. Hear how it even stumbles the rhythmic breathing of embalmed men.

The heroes of this moment were raised by police from their beds by the alarm at one o'clock. The keeper had found the Volvo with its deeply scratched side still there in the dark, the sandwich box left behind on the passenger seat. Half of the company wait at the bottom of the hill, for news. Now, even without the crackling radio, they know the man is found and alive.

As the sun begins its rise, the mists follow, and so do human hearts. The lower party echo to the sky their own deep cry of joy. It leaps even higher than the first, dancing between the peaks and floating beyond, to the furthest crest of my realm. And feel, my dear, how it reverberates too in the ponderous rock deep below, how the very Earth threatens to grunt and rumble and roll over beneath them. Forgive this gravel in my throat. It's nothing. A residue of winter chill.

Dawn is bringing its dewy light and you, my dear, are defeated for another season. Until Samhain then, when we shall feel your blue face and white frosted hair near again, the shivered wings of your host of herons. Then you can score new scars onto the hill, and clutch again at human hearts.

Now go!

Orange Twine

'THAT MANY THINGS on a farm are answered by this stuff,' Dan said.

Jill watched him wind a length of bristly orange baling twine between two gates to make an enclosure. When he swung the gate open for them, the ewe and her new lamb crackled onto the clean bed of straw.

She leant over the gate and tickled the ewe's head. The fleece felt greasy and soft. 'Sweet,' she said.

'Eh?' he leaned the side of his head towards her. 'You speak that bloody quiet.'

'So sweet. That's all,' Jill said.

Dan leant in and gave the ewe a nudge, pushed the lamb's tail-end so it was pointing its nose up towards the udder. Its black legs were all splayed out but at least they were holding it up now.

'Softy, eh?' he said.

Jill saw that he had grown man's hands—big, calloused and workish, grained with dirt. But they were still gentle on the animals.

Dan had been here every Easter when she visited, just a few years ahead of her, a bit like a brother might be, she supposed. Under his baseball cap, his face was tanned from the weeks of Easter sunshine. She watched him close the gate and tie a second knot of orange to keep the sheep in. Something about his hands made her feel funny, like wanting to look, but wanting to look away all at the same time.

'See,' he said, standing up from the gate and pointing at his boot laced at the ankle with orange. 'Boot laces. Light switch.' He pulled at the dangling orange twine that led to a bare bulb in the ceiling of the barn. 'And belt.' With a big grin, he pulled up his shirt and showed her his waist, the jeans cinched through the belt loops with baling twine.

She saw the bare skin of his belly and pretended to scratch her ear, so her hand covered part of her cheek.

He dropped his shirt.

'We use it loads too,' she said, after a pause. She pulled her T-shirt downwards. It gave her hands something to do. She'd also seen in the mirror how it made it look almost as if she had tits.

'Aye?'

'At the stables. For mending hay nets. And we tether the ponies with it, in case they pull back. It snaps,' she

123

explained, finding her confidence now, 'rather than hurting them if the head collar digs in. Or breaking the head collar. Because they're expensive.'

Jill's mother got furious with her for coming home every Saturday evening in the winter months with pockets full of the stuff. It got all caught up with sweetie wrappers and bits of hay. Her mother had to throw it out before Jill's clothes went in the washing machine. Apparently it brought hay into the bloody house, and hay belonged outside.

'You've finally got a pony, then?' Dan asked.

'Not my own. I help out at the stables.' Then she corrected herself. '*Work* there.'

Each weekend as they approached the stables on the bumpy track, the excitement would bubble up in her— before Brian released her from the air conditioned, silent, smoky world of his car.

She didn't tell Dan how she could have been going to the stables every day during the holiday, instead of this long, empty stay at her grandma's in the middle of nowhere. She might even have taken a sleeping bag and stayed over in the tack room. She didn't mention to Dan how she thought enviously of the other girls today—arriving with sandwich boxes, and their leather whips.

'I ride Lightning,' she said, as if that made him more hers, and more present. 'I look after him. He's cool.'

The thought of who might be combing the knots out of Lightning's shiny black mane and buffing his hind quarters with a body brush, made her want to wee. Or there was something tight and tingling down there, if she thought about it too much anyway.

'So you're Thunder, eh?' He sat sideways on the quad bike, one foot raised on the wheel arch, grinning. He took out a packet of cigarettes. As he put one in his mouth, she thought he hesitated, as if about to offer her one. But then he stuffed them back into his shirt pocket. She hadn't seen him smoke before, looked over her shoulder, wondered if his mother knew about it.

'So, what's cool about him? This Lightning. Fast, is he?'

She nodded, 'Gentle too, though'. She didn't mention the fact she could only ride him once a fortnight because that's all her mum could afford, or how she'd overheard Brian use the f-word when her mum had told him how much it cost.

'You don't want to spoil her,' was what he had said.

One of the OK things about coming here were the big bare green hills. She could walk for ever. If she tried to walk at home, there were always big boys who fired potato guns and bad words at her. There were tunnels under the roads with dogs in them, and people with dark faces. Up here in these hills, she could ride Lightning for as long as she liked, in secret. She would give him his head and gallop flat out —a streak across the skyline, Lightning snorting and pounding under her.

In the long afternoons, if she stayed in the cottage while

her grandma napped, she put the TV on as she straddled the arm of the big corduroy sofa, flung reins over a wheelback chair in front of it, and rode for Scotland. Her crotch would slide rhythmically along the sofa arm—Lightning's bare back—as she sat the bucks, guided him over jumps and swam with him through flooding rivers. It was so good it tingled.

She dreaded the days when it rained at the stables. If rides got cancelled, they would all be stuck in the tack room together, and the older girls would tell gross stories about boyfriends or get the younger ones to do things they didn't want to do. Sometimes they sent Jill to the corner shop to buy cigarettes. She always got laughed at by the shopkeeper, it was so obvious she wasn't sixteen, and she would come back empty-handed and drenched to the skin.

Recently they'd been trying to get Jill and the younger ones to faint. Standing in one of the stables, a girl would squeeze the air out of you from behind, and then lower you onto the straw, speaking gobbledegook into your ear. Or they'd sling a leading rein over the beam in the tack room, place a chair under it and get you to stand on it with your neck caught in the noose. The chair was pulled away, then put back quickly before you really floundered, before you hanged.

It was best to avoid the place if it rained. Or at least keep out of the tack room and go and talk to Lightning while he munched his hay.

Dan was tugging a loop of baling twine in his hands. 'You say it snaps, eh?' he said. Takes a bit to break this stuff. Strong as f...'

She felt the tingle of agreement in her hands. When she lifted hay bales at the stables, she would clinch the two strands of twine in one hand, and the bale would bang against her legs as she carried it out to the field.

'Slave labour,' she'd heard Brian mutter when he'd come too early to collect her one evening, and watched her grappling with the weight of a bale. He'd seen afterwards the two long red dents on her bare hands.

Dan swung onto the quad bike. The engine rattled. He stood tall on the foot pegs as he reversed it, and then zoomed forward, over the sun-baked, rutted track, waving goodbye at her. And she was left alone watching the ewes and their lambs.

On the top of the hill, on its very highest point, there was a sharp blue breeze that cooled the sweat under her T-shirt as her lungs calmed down after the climb. The sky seemed to arc huge over her and she turned on her axis and took in the full compass of the hills.

The pointy shape over there she knew as Tinto Hill. Her mum had taken her up it for a picnic. Before Brian. Since then, Jill got packaged off to her grandma's alone. Another turn, and she stared up to the summit pronged with its three antennae. Tucked below it was the farm and her grandma's cottage hidden by the dark strip of forest. She couldn't see it, but knew that underneath the green canopy of trees, rabbits with bobtails bounced about, and there was a heap of wood offcuts getting ready for a bonfire, and black plastic that flapped and ghosted in the wind at night. She turned again. On the main road, trucks pulled great flat rectangles of shadow towards England.

She lay down on her back in the grass, out of the cool cut of the wind, and watched some black and white birds scudding above her.

'Rest,' she said to Lightning, who she could trust to graze nearby with his reins loose on his neck. He was loyal —would stay close by without her holding him. Every now and again he pricked his head up to listen for something. Horses were ace at listening. You could talk and talk to them, quietly in the stall, straight into the furry lining of their long ears. You could tell they were listening hard because they didn't muck about.

There was a bald patch exactly on the summit of the hill, and on it lay a charred log which had been burnt into a strange shape—like the head of a big bird. It made her think of one of those beaked dinosaur things. She sat up and cupped it in her hands. When she put it down again she saw that her hands were black. Instead of wiping them on the grass, an impulse took them to her face where she smeared a line on each cheek.

She let Lightning have his head so he could pick his

own way back down the steep hill. When they got to the flat field at the bottom, she gathered up the reins and galloped him hard towards the wide ditch, urging him on with her voice and legs and the grinding of her bum, just as she'd been taught, and yelling 'hup!' as they took off. She thrust herself forward, soaring over the ditch, and then pulled him back into a collected canter, circling and controlled. She didn't like to gallop him too much. The ground was like rock after all this dry weather. It could jar his legs. They dropped back to an extended walk, working on a loose rein, just as Robbie, her instructor, insisted they did at the end of a jumping session, to cool down.

Robbie had looked at her in a long smirking way recently. It made her stare straight ahead as she rode around him in a circle.

'You're going to be trouble, aren't you? Legs up to your armpits,' he'd said. And when she'd misjudged a jump, and landed, painfully, on the pommel of the saddle, he'd shrieked, 'Lost something, have you Jill?'

But she didn't know what he meant and had felt confused, as if she was supposed to have dropped something, and she said, 'No.'

'Not already lost it?' he seemed to be pretending shock. She couldn't think of a reply.

She became aware of the quad bike crossing the next field, and then coming towards her. Lightning vanished. She dropped her hands from the reins, let them fall to her sides, pulling at her T-shirt. She knelt on the grass, pluck-ing daisies into a pile, and pretended surprise when Dan greeted her and turned off the engine.

'Hi, Thunder. What's with the face?' He mimed two swipes across his cheeks.

She wiped at her face with spit on the back of her hand and waved vaguely back in the direction of the hill.

'Been up there?'

She nodded, colour rising at the thought he'd seen her galloping with her hands held out in front of her, and heard all that shouting.

'What you doing?'

'Making a necklace,' she said, absorbed by trying to insert a stalk into the narrow incision made by her thumb-nail.

'Daisy chaining. At your age.'

She dropped the daisies, ashamed of her childishness. When she looked up at him, she saw a wry grin and won-dered if he'd meant something she hadn't understood.

'Grow up fast these days,' he said. 'So you've been up Gallow Law the day.'

'Where?'

He nodded up at the hill. 'That yin.'

'Yes.'

'Used to have fires up there.'

'Why?'

He shrugged. 'Protection'.

'From what?'

'Witches. Disease. Thunder and lightning'. He laughed. 'In the old days.'

She remained puzzled. In the past she and Dan had played together easily despite the difference in their ages. But it all suddenly seemed complicated and confusing.

'Seen who I've got in here?' Dan pulled at his jacket zip.

She stood up. A small white head appeared against his chest.

'Oooh.' Her hand shot out towards the lamb, but retreated again before she made contact. She pulled at her T-shirt.

'Stroke it if you want.'

Her hand went out again and touched the soft head, but her face blazed. Her hand was too close to the hollow at the bottom of Dan's neck. It made her think of Brian and how hair seemed to crawl up and out of his shirts, like it did from his nostrils.

'Mother rejected it,' Dan said.

'Why?'

'They do sometimes. Or the mothers die.'

'What from?'

'The birth. Disease. Whatever.'

'Poor thing,' she whispered to its soft ear.

'Aye,' Dan said, and patted at the top of its head. She wished, suddenly, that she was the lamb curled up against his chest, all safe, and rescued and warm.

The sun was sinking behind the strip of forest when she walked back down the track to the cottage. It made a dark green pool in which new lambs fizzed about while their mothers grazed nearby. She felt like skipping and didn't care who saw her.

The next afternoon, her grandma napped as usual, and Jill mounted the sofa arm. She was distracted from Lightning and water jumps by a dark-haired woman in black and white on the TV, slowly approaching a man. She undid his tie and used it to pull his head down to her, into a kiss that seemed to go on and on.

The 'reins' that Jill used around the chair back became a tie. Closing her eyes as the woman had done, she tipped the chair towards her face, till her mouth touched the smooth hard rail of its back. She gathered her lips into a full cushion, and kissed. She kissed the broad coroneted brow between Lightning's eyes, and she kissed Dan's smiling tanned face, at one and the same time.

She practised and practised all afternoon.

When she got into the yard the next morning, all was quiet. The quad was parked up, and she looked for Dan in the barn and out where the hay bales were kept. She passed the rusty tractor, the trailer with only one wheel, the pile of tyres. Then something white and fluffy caught her eye. It was too big for a lamb. A mound of fleece on its side, its back to her.

'Ah, sweet,' she thought. 'Sleeping'.

But as she got closer, she saw that there was something too still about it. Its legs were stiff and straight. Did Dan realise, she wondered. Could he save it if she could find him and let him know?

But as she crept closer, something else caught her eye. A tail of orange twine led from the ewe's neck. And she could see a dent in the fleece where it had been pulled tight. The ewe had been noosed, lassoed with baling twine.

'Thunder!' Dan was suddenly behind her. 'Looking for lambs?'

'What happened?' She pointed at the hung sheep.

'Casualty. Last night.'

'Why . . . why has it got baling twine..'

He shrugged. 'Had to get it off the hill.'

She stared at Dan.

'Behind the quad bike,' he said.

She still stared.

'I dragged it down.'

Tears pricked behind her eyes. She thought of the hard ground, of all the ruts and bumps the poor soft ewe must have bounced over.

He laughed. 'It was dead already.'

For the first time his laugh sounded rough and smoky,

133

like Brian's. Perhaps he had hairy nostrils too, that she had never noticed. Her attempt to make sense of it, of him, felt like a twisted coil of twine in her pocket, caught up with biros or paper and bits of hay, and impossible to pull back to the simple loop it had started with.

She pulled down her T-shirt. She pulled at it so there was something for her hands to do whilst she fought with her tears. The T-shirt was taut under the arms of the jacket tied around her waist. She saw Dan look. He looked there, at her tits, or where they should be. He held his gaze there, and then looked up at her face, grinning.

No words came. She turned away and ran back down the track towards the cottage. A few drops of rain spat onto her hot face and she slowed to a walk. She put her jacket back on, and thrust her hands deep into her hay-filled pockets.

Le Grand Jeté

SHE BOWS AT the front of the stage, triumphant and composed, arms raised like wings behind her. The crowd's memory of her still spins and spins, following the orchestra's thrilling close. Her lips are painted theatre-red to prod hot pokers into her father's guts. But naturally, he does not stand beside me. Nor will he be found in any theatre emblazoned with her name.

I'm on my feet with the roaring audience, choking for her 'Giselle'. For the sweet injustice of her heartbreak and death. For the wedding she never had. For the moonlit gaslit forest haunted by the dancing of white maidens.

My hands slap, together and back, together and back, till they smart brick-red. Then she's gone—the broad brow, bold raven's head, proud chin. The final curtain still sways a little, teased by the after-shock of her soaring dance.

I dare not look at my fellows. The shadow clings to me too closely as yet.

A different clamour is before me now.

This rattling, stamping dragon of a machine draws me back, after the men have finished their shift, and the gas lights are dimmed. I hover over it, watching the flicking leather straps, the hurtling shuttle, its velocity caught and recaught, back and forth.

Outside in its brick built lair, the steam engine huffs and puffs. Ropes groan around the flywheel, converting fire to woollen cloth. Even after all these years, it remains a small miracle. I laugh as the cloth rolls inch by inch onto the beam at my knees. But my laughter is swallowed by the clickety-clack, kershunk, kershunk, kershunk, that shakes the building.

'Will the walls burst?' She asked, when she first heard it.

She watched the loom with parted lips, cheeks bright, as if she saw a merry-go-round, not a thing of industry. Her hands were over her ears, saving them for another kind of music. But the oil-slicked slide of wood and metal stretched wide her eyes.

'Faster than you can run, Lucia,' I shouted. On a previous visit, when she was more girl, less woman, her feet had swooped her across the moor above the Mill, her dress sailing behind her in the wind. She was like a bird, thrilled at its own ability to glide and turn, indulging for the joy of it. Until Signore La Catena, her father, had bellowed her back.

He focussed his twisted frown on the heaving warp threads lifting and separating alternately to clear the shuttle's path. He gave no sign that he was impressed by the new machine, but I knew that the spectacle alone, and his daughter's springs of excitement by his side, would secure an order twice as large as normal. And with this new machine, I could damn well deliver it to the man.

We went next to the engine house. The heat embraced us, dampened her skin to a slight sheen. We watched the gleaming monster that chugged and pumped.

'Is like a chapel,' she said.

I looked at the high arched windows and the vaulted ceiling, and nodded at her, though this conformity prickled me.

'Do you worship?' She pointed at the steam engine, and then her eye was dancing and black, catching off me, her father, John Banville who was stoking the boiler. Her laughter followed it like a flying sprite through door and window.

'Is all yours?' She pointed at the rough-hewn stones from which my new weaving shed had been built, at the machines which beat down towards the centre of the Earth. Through the window of the engine shed, the Mill loomed. The chimney huffed up smoke, meshing with the outpourings of the other mills to cap the town with a yellowish brooding vapour.

'It's my father's,' I said. 'But it will be mine.'

I pointed out other things. The pirn-winders carrying their baskets up and down the stairs, and Joe Kyle caught in silhouette through the third floor window, moving backwards and forwards with the carriage of spindles on the Mule as if they were joined in some grand bucolic square dance.

'Such weight,' she said, then sprang into the air, hanging there for a moment, stretched to the sky. Her skirts puffed dust across the floor when she landed. Her laughter rose again, and the Signore's hand clamped onto her shoulder, stilling and steadying.

'She has the same spirit as when she was so high,' I said to him, holding my hand at the height of a ten-year old's head. But his frown only deepened.

'You like new things, modern ways,' she said to me.

'The first power looms in this town,' I agreed. 'But I find new ways for the men too. I won't have them displaced by machines.'

'You are like a dancer who makes the dance as he goes,' she said.

My cheeks glowed as if I was a boy.

At Crimsworth Hall, we waltzed, along with mill-owners and fine girls who came chaperoned by their mothers. At first, I could not dumb the looms. They clickety-clacked in my head above the orchestra's one two three, one two three. My steps were heavy and hesitant, but they lightened as she set the rhythm, raised her smile to me. Her skirts swirled at her ankles as we turned. It made me breathe more quickly, this extravagance of movement, my self-surprise at what the gangle of my body seemed to permit. With her.

I was certain that she led me beyond the normal bounds of the waltz into experiment. There were dangerous, unbalanced moves which threw laughter from us. Sheer speed span and rattled us between the glissades of the other couples.

We passed into the cool dining room.

'You are one of those spirit maidens,' I told her. 'From Slav legend. Who dance men to their death. Tell me it is so, for I can think of no better way to die.'

Her laugh shot from her mouth as a sleek blackbird, soaring to the ceiling before its echo fluttered eave to eave, against floor and ceiling.

Her father approached, his wild frown seeking us.

'Lucia must rest now.'

'Papà. . . ?'

'It is I who am short of breath,' I laughed. 'She is untouched.'

'Good night, Mr Hunsden.' He took her arm and linked her out into the night.

The next day he came to the Mill alone.

'She is resting,' he said. 'Last night was too vigorous.'

I laughed loud and long.

'She is a woman,' he said. 'A young woman.'

Which made me laugh again. 'And women surely dance the best.'

'She gets wrong ideas. She wishes to learn this new thing they talk about, like Carlotta Grisi, this ballet d'action, these women who dance with fire in the heart. Fire in the body. It is pagan.'

'She has talent.'

'She wants to go to La Scala, Paris Opera, Vienna.'

'And why not? She has the energy.'

He looked at me as if I was a surprise bull in a meadow where he was picnicking, and had assumed himself to be safe. A mixture of indignation, anger and fear screwed up his gnarled face.

'You wish for her the life of a dancer?'

'I wish for her the life she wishes.'

He faced me, and I saw Lucia's black eyes. But they were bolted onto me, not like hers that glistered and flitted from one thing to the next.

'Are you sure, Mr Hunsden,' he said slowly. I saw the jerk and fall of his Adam's apple before he spoke again. 'Are you sure you wish for her never to marry?'

Our eyes stayed connected while I paused. A breath was left untaken. I saw what her rebellion might mean, and dredged up the purest belief I could find.

'No man should contain her.'

His hand slammed down on the bolt of cloth we were bargaining over. A small cloud of loose fibres leapt into the sunlight that beamed through glass, making me cough and my eyes water. His head bent towards the finishing table. I saw that something convulsed his stomach. His shoulders rolled forward rhythmically, twice or three times.

'If her mother should know this, from the tomb . . .' he started. 'If her mother would see her in this 'Cuchacha', this Gypsy she wishes to play, in black lace and pink satin . . .'

His eyes were coal hot when he raised them to me again.

The three of us went back to the loom before they left for Italy, to see the dancing shuttle, its crash and shlock and schlick, the dragon snorting oily and black and shaking its cast iron frame. I saw how the movement and speed captivated her again. She walked around it, observing the couplings which transferred the power, the beam at the back which inched out the warp threads, restraining them with a weighted chain.

She was at the unguarded side of the loom, hands over her ears, that smile flickering again.

'Get away!' Muted by the noise, I motioned her out of the shuttle's path, grabbed at her wrist. But she evaded me, hands jumping back from me in mock surprise, a glitter in her eyes, her chin challenging.

I grabbed again at her, this time caught her waist and scooped her to safety at my side. A great crack shot across the room, filling our ears, and the loom went silent. I stilled the drive-wheel. Lucia looked around the weaving shed in confusion.

'It has come out? Escaped?' Her eyes were wide at its impudence.

'That's why you mustn't stand in its path,' I said, indicating the torn and splintered box it had burst through.

Her father and I watched her step the oil-soaked boards as she went to the far side of the weaving shed to look for the shuttle. She was illuminated as if by floodlight under the saw-toothed roof.

She walked back towards me, her finger tracing the bullet-tipped nose of the shuttle, blackening the tips of her white-gloved fingers. She placed it into my hands and her eyes were still on me, her chin jutting and square, wanting to know more.

'It can kill a man,' I said.

'You saved me?'

'Yes.'

'But it travels so far.' She waved a hand. 'Is beautiful.' She was almost laughing.

'That's in its nature, if it gets away.'

I thought of all the power that John Banville stoked each day, how it forged on through steam and rope and pulleys and straps, to hurl the shuttle. And I thought of the task for which that force was captured. To make drab cloth for uniforms.

'You prefer it to take flight?' I asked.

She nodded. 'Is more exciting, no?'

I held her gaze. And then we were both laughing, and her father puzzled his frown at us. She refused his arm and took mine as we left the weaving shed.

'You saved me,' she said again. Her eyes seemed hard and determined.

I squeezed the Signore's shoulder and Lucia left my arm. Later that day a downy softness whispered past me. I pictured myself casting her, part airborne already, into a huge leap, one leg leading, the other straight and following. Her arms extended into the unknown. She arced out of the grime of industry towards forests, lakes, a spirit world, in floating white tulle.

The next time I saw her she had landed on the stage at La Scala, Milan and her toes made the briefest contact with the earth before she flew once more.

~

Refusing to be weighed down absolutely by buildings and chugging machinery and bolts of cloth, I travel widely now, when Mill business allows. She has bewitched me to do so. Vienna, Paris, Munich, St Petersburg. I haunt the places where velvet curtains swoop. For two hours I am spellbound, as I watch her fly and leap, spinning stories. And then the curtain plunges once more.

She must know that I follow her career from box to box across the continent, clapping till my hands smart. She must feel my hawk eyes on her, for last year the postman brought a small package. Her face had been stilled into an ivory miniature, her name inscribed on the back.

I keep it in my pocket to remind me of the real woman she has become. Sometimes, late at night, I take it out and turn it in the firelight, or hold it under a beam of unclouded moonlight as I walk in Hunsden Wood. And sometimes the sight of it casts a feathery shadow.

Reclaimed Land

'WHAT DO YOU think the answer is?' she asked Ken. She leant close, aware that her accent and her expression of puzzlement would mark her out as a visitor, an alien trying to learn the rules. 'When they ask "how are you" like that?'

'What's so difficult?' he laughed.

'The way they emphasise the middle word. It sounds so sincere, as if they know you already.' She found it strange how a common language didn't stop things feeling foreign.

'And?'

'They've only just clapped eyes on you. And there's a queue behind. You're not going to get to be best pals, are you?'

'Just naturally friendly, I guess.'

'So, do I tell them about the arthritis in my pinkie, and the fact I didn't get much sleep last night?' Cath squeezed

145

his thigh. 'Thanks to someone.'

'I'm sure they'd love to hear,' he turned towards her. 'Especially what you seem to like so much, when I . . .'

'Ken.' She made owl eyes at him, but the recollection slithered up her soft belly, pulling a flush with it, to her face.

'Wild thing.' He smiled at her, his mouth slightly squint, crinkling at the corners, pulling her fingers to it. 'This city agrees with you, eh?' He took her thumb into his mouth and sucked.

The people and furniture and traffic on the periphery of her vision blurred. The 'thing' was awakening again like an insatiable sea serpent thrashing in her gut. There would be tonight, she thought, and two further nights after that to ensure it was well-nourished.

As Ken opened his magazine, she stared out onto Broadway over her huge cardboard cup of cappuccino. He'd wanted the Starbucks experience, even though, just as she had said, it was exactly the same as the one at home in Edinburgh. That was the point of course, you know what you're getting, wherever you find them in the world.

In the office doorways opposite, huddles of smokers were reduced to cockroaches, curled into their hard-shell-backed shivers, cursing Bloomberg for banishing them from their own workplace. A man from the 'Clean Team' was directly outside the café , sweeping the pavement. Or perhaps the 'sidewalk'. She was absorbing the new language, her native resistance polished thin by the good-humoured insistence around her. Restroom, store, subway, sidewalk. She could say them all now.

She leafed through *Time Out*. Just on one weekday night there seemed to be a thousand things you could do in cafés, bars and bookshops to increase your understanding of the world. Arundhati Roy was leading a public discussion on US Foreign Policy; a journalist was talking about a new book on the Middle East Conflict; there were numerous readings of Persian, Russian, Japanese literature. If she had come here with Shona, they would have been out every hour of the day queuing for a different event, on a kind of social justice pilgrimage. But Cath hadn't phoned Shona in ages. It seemed like a distant, long-ago kind of life, the worthiness and campaigning, that she would look back on with nostalgia.

The streets stretched, taut like guitar strings up and down Manhattan Island. All the debris—blossom petals, cigarette ends, paper flyers for shows—was gusting along with the flurried migration of feet, north and south. Head down, the 'Clean Team' man was absorbed by his task, scurrying against the tide, armed with a white baseball cap, a bucket on wheels, and a long-handled broom. Of course, she noted, he was black.

Above them, on the building across the street, a bank of screens came to life. A company, Bugg Brothers, processed its name across one of them.

'Look,' she said to Ken, as a monstrous wave built across the screens, rearing up to a stasis at full height. Although the car horns, shouts, road work throb, bus growls, brake squeals, insisted they were far from natural disaster, it looked as if the wave would swell across Broadway, break over them, swamp the street, inundate Starbucks, wash them all out into the Hudson River. Their bodies would be separated from their cardboard cups, high plastic-cushioned stools, white napkins. The girl next to Ken would lose her brick-like hardback only half read, the workman next to her would lose his hard hat. He might even lose the cell phone, into which he'd just signed off, 'I love you, baby.'

The wave dropped and curled back down, remaining two-dimensional, restraining itself to the other side of the street.

'Huh,' said Ken.

BUGG BROTHERS paraded past again, words in a controlled electronic procession. It was just business, Cath thought, technology, lights, and trickery. Not a force of nature at all.

They walked north, his hand on her waist, the day warming now as the sun burnt through spring mist. Yellow cabs dominated the traffic. She noticed one with a roof-top commercial carrying a sultry, ringletted black girl, a bare leg showing. RENT it said. She tutted inwardly.

Snorts of steam escaped from the underworld of the city, just as she'd seen on the movies. Her light skirt lifted as she walked over a vent, sending a breeze ruffling up her inner thighs, almost touching her there, with a tip of tongue or tail. She smiled at Ken and let the skirt whisper back down to her knees in its own time.

Despite her collusion with them, the hot breaths which punctuated the streets were slightly unsettling. They seemed to threaten a reversal of order, as if the cars, the yellow cabs, that man with his bright pink suede shoes, and they themselves, were being bucked on the back of some unseen monster which was merely tolerating them. What if their lives tickled its spine into a mighty shake, she wondered—would they be lost in a chaotic eruption of heat and steam?

'Did I tell you I'm gonna get my hair painted red?' she snatched at a passing conversation between two youths. 'Like I'll be one of those people no one speaks to.'

'That's fucking shit, man,' someone spat into his cell phone.

'Walk. Don't walk,' the streets commanded. No one obeyed.

As they went through the Columbus Circle gate, a smiling woman told her cell phone, 'I'm in Central Park and everything reminds me of you.' Cath stifled a laugh. A few paces on, she wondered if she could ever be capable of such casual emotional honesty.

149

It was suddenly a hot day, and they walked slowly. They had to, because of the dogs. They waded through poodles, retrievers, dogs with big jowls, dogs wearing red coats. On the grass, a pair frisked over and around each other with wide drooling grins, not baring teeth, growling and fighting as they would in a park at home. Their newly-bonded owners stood with paper mugs of coffee, leads and sticks in their hands, their talk tumbling as freely as their animals.

'Let's sit down, just for a minute,' Cath said, and they sat watching. She blinked into the sun, he avoided the dazzle behind his shades. 'I need to decide,' she said, 'if I'm going to apply for that job when I get back.'

'You don't know when you're onto a good thing. Long holidays, small classes.'

'I know. But it's never felt right to me—teaching children of the privileged.'

'Big drop in pay.'

'I know. And no more long weekends.'

'That's no good, is it?' He kissed her ear and she turned her mouth onto his.

In the Museo del Barrio, she lost Ken for a little so that she was alone, with only the sleepy security guard at the threshold of the room, when she found the first painting, the one called *Maternidad*, completed in 1959. The young pregnant woman stood in a room. She wore a turquoise shift dress and held a wide red cup near her chest. She was barefoot, bare-armed, her hair tied back, head slightly turned away from the viewer towards a small table set for two. A curl of water melon waited on a plate. Above the table an upward arc of yellow light illuminated a picture of a mother hugging a child, and a shelf of books with different coloured spines. She felt the love flow from the painter to the woman, the brush marks edgy and flat, the woman beautiful. It told so simply how they both expected, as if her hand and the painter's were joined on her swelling belly.

A hot breath lifted the hair from her ear, teeth nipped her neck, his groin pressed into her from behind. She smiled. He slipped a hand around her waist, and the serpent writhed with a ferocious slam inside her, threatening to double her over. Ken had surely felt it too, thrusting into his hand. She felt herself as the woman in the painting—loved, desired. And how would it feel to be pregnant too? She'd only ever thought of pregnant women before as asexual, maternal in shapeless clothes.

'We're quite near the hotel here, aren't we?' he whispered, his belly-stroking hand rumpling her skirt, lifting it up the front of her legs slightly.

'A wee rest before dinner might be sensible, mightn't it?' she answered, half turning.

They heard the shuffling feet of the security guard

behind them, checking the room, and her skirt slipped back into place.

She stared at the painting.

'I love his work,' she said.

'"Painter of the people". What's that all about?'

'He cared about people. In Puerto Rica. He had a social conscience.'

'Let's think,' he screwed up his eyes. 'Social conscience. That means cutting off the dandelion heads before the seeds explode into your neighbour's garden. Right?'

'Maybe where you come from. Very noble.'

'Oh, not me, I like dandelions. A bit of colour about the place.'

'They breed like fuck, though,' she said.

'Mmm,' he pulled her towards him again, then dropped his hold on her, and took her hand, ready to lead her out of the museum, to bed.

'Wait,' she said, checking herself. 'There's still one more room.'

'Five minutes, right?' He shook a finger at her.

'Where are you going?'

'There's a shop, isn't there?'

'Haven't you had enough of rampant consumerism?'

'Not yet,' and he walked towards the shop doorway. From around the corner she heard a loud woman's voice, 'So what's Madonna got to do with *any*thing.'

At 86th Street, on their way to the museum, they had waited for the uptown subway.

'Only goes to Harlem or the Bronx,' he'd said. The names seemed to rattle in his mouth as if he could taste their notoriety.

They looked at the subway map with its snaking tracks of red, yellow, green. 'That's right,' she said. 'That's the right direction.'

He'd whistled through his teeth, and seemed to grip the handles of his shopping bags tighter as the platform filled with black teenagers on their way home from school. The girls' bums were taut inside jeans. The boys, in ragged groups, wore long plain white T-shirts over their baggy trousers. They were man-sized boys, fresh-faced, but thick-limbed, so that they shrank the cave of the subway. It squeezed in on the waiting crowd. Ken's face had started to look set as he craned down the track looking for the train. The longer it took to come, the more firmly they were crushed in the sunken heat.

'Maybe we should get a cab,' he said.

Her reply was swallowed by the boom of the approaching train, and they'd crammed in through the opening door. She giggled as they got pressed together, face to face. But he put the bags between their feet and kept looking around him. When they emerged back into daylight, he peered into the bags, as if to check that the Diesel shirts and the clutch of CDs hadn't escaped.

It was the colours of a print that seized her next, a poster that Rafael Tufiño had designed to celebrate the 25th anniversary of the Division of Community Education. Purple, turquoise, orange, pink—the flat bold shirts worn by the circle of people who sat on wheel-backed chairs in a pool of sunlit grass. Men wore black-banded Panama hats, a woman held a closed umbrella, fluted pink and purple. It gave a tropical spin to the vibrant precision she'd seen on a holiday in the Alps—a meadow of Gentians, Yellow Oxe-Eyes, and Pinks under a clear Swiss sun.

But it wasn't just the colours that grabbed at her. Each person held a sheet of paper. The simple flat shapes of their backs, the incline of their heads towards the paper, told of attention and respect. Behind them were bushes with bright flowers, and the emergent shapes of the house-shacks of their village. This was why he was called 'Pintor del Pueblo'. What a celebration in two dimensions, a vision of community, of development.

'That's ten,' a voice chipped at her.

'Ten what?' she turned to Ken, and rode the kick that jabbed at her insides, when she saw the tanned face, the shades pushed up onto his head, that smile.

'Minutes.' He put his hand onto the back of her neck, under her hair, and moved his fingers there.

'Don't distract me.' She turned back to the picture.

'Are you there, Uncle Alfred?' he quavered in her ear, looking at the circle of chairs.

'It's perfect, isn't it? You could never get that across in words. Peasant politics. Democracy.'

'Are you allowed to call them peasants?' He rested his chin on her shoulder, and when she didn't answer, said, 'So it's not a seance then?'

She stared hard at the picture, wanting to imprint its brilliance into her mind, be able to recall it when she needed inspiration.

'I remember that, at primary school,' he said. 'We were allowed to have a class outside sometimes. On the one day the sun shined, I suppose.'

'It's more than an outdoor classroom,' she said. 'These are the kind of people I want to teach.'

'Is it true, do you think,' he wrapped his arms around her and opened his mouth on her cheek, 'that sunshine makes you horny.' She felt the tickle of his spiky hair, his soap smell. His hand reached up inside her T-shirt and began to tease at her nipple, firing blood up and down the deep hidden passages of her body. She had to close her eyes. She wanted to run fingers over the flinching skin around his belly button, to arch her back as she clung hard to his bare shoulders.

'Not everyone in this world can be well off,' he said.

She hardly heard, just felt an opening, a softening, her knees buckling. She tipped her head so he could bite at her neck. Her hand slipped backwards onto his thigh. She knew that a window-rattling orgasm was lurking inside

155

her, waiting to be unleashed.

'Hair shirt doesn't suit you,' he said, his hand between her shoulder blades, tickling.

His arm brushed the stub of magazine poking from her bag, and it fell with a loud slap onto the floor. She dislodged him to lean down and retrieve it. It was folded open at the page of listings on which she'd circled Arundhati Roy's name. She noticed it was against today's date, 7 p.m. She pushed the magazine back into her bag.

His body surrounded hers again, sucking her close. His chin felt heavy and sharp on her shoulder. It was hard to breathe. She looked up at Tufiño's picture—the colours passionate with tropical heat, the concentration of the figures dedicated to improvement, to self-help. She thought of Shona. At this very moment she was probably raising money for flood or earthquake victims. Cath didn't even know where in the world the disasters might be, right now.

The struggle materialised as a twist in her upper body. It rose up into her arm, into a fist ball which she pushed against Ken's chest, thrusting him away. It surprised with its strength.

'Fuck off,' she spurted.

Her voice shattered the clinging, soft thing that the room had become around them. It sent paintings back to rectangular parallel hangings on a crisp white wall. The ceiling rose a couple of feet, and footsteps clashed on the wooden floor in the next room. She smelt wax polish and coffee. The security guard returned to his slump in the doorway. As Cath recovered her surroundings, she seemed to reclaim some submerged remnants of herself.

Ken laughed, releasing his hands from her as if he'd just discovered that the plum he'd picked was actually a slug.

'I'm definitely going to apply for it.' She turned back to the painting. 'I can't think straight when you're doing that.'

'That's why you like it.' His arms were folded.

'I can't think like me.'

'What made you think of that now, anyway. The job?' His voice had acquired a sharp edge. 'When you're supposed to be on holiday.'

'The painting.'

'How?'

Words clogged in her throat, unable to find the right order for a common language between them.

She shrugged.

'We'd better go, sweetie,' he whispered. 'I think you need a wee rest.'

As they walked into the early evening crowds commuting north and south along the island, she pulled her bag close to her so that the rolled magazine wouldn't jab at passers-by. She took care to step around the hot breaths that reached up at her from the vents in the sidewalk.

When they got to the bottom of the hotel steps, the porter swung open the door, ready for them. A flash of river and sky reflected off it. Cath hesitated, and Ken pushed his shades onto the top of his head.

'You go on,' she said. 'I'll see you later.'

She turned back into the crowd as Ken climbed the steps. As she walked away she heard the porter say, 'How are you, sir?'

'How *are* you,' came Ken's faint reply.

Night's High Noon

IT'S ALREADY 11 p.m. and the contest has only twenty-four hours to go, when I see her appear through the white wall of haar. She's patrolling the silver strip of shallows; beyond it is the russet seaweed that crusted in the sun today before the screen dropped to mask the Hoy Hills. I watch her silhouette moving through the mist. Her long hair is damped flat, and she wears waders, the chest-high ones. But she doesn't wear a life jacket. So very foolish.

I am in my camouflage and crouch, sweaty and breathless, in one of the wartime look-outs. These shores are riddled like a catacomb—the shells of these concrete bunkers and then deeper and darker, grown into the ground, the Neolithic chambered cairns. I've crawled through many of them this week. One needs a break sometimes from searching the water, and from the scorch of the sun.

I watch her pause and face the sea. A small dark shape

159

dangles beneath her hand, and as she mutters, it begins to swing and spin. So. She's part of the contest too. But she'll never find it that way. She gets her 'answer' from the pendulum and wades straight out, paling as she makes small splashes and ripples, stirring the glass sea. She leaves in my mind a picture of a pre-Raphaelite maiden gripping the sides of a boat in an ecstasy of expectation as she's propelled out in it, and is swallowed into the blank white stare of sea or sky. And of course, she has no oars.

Ha, but this is the midsummer raving in my imagination. You hear it about people here, how the blackbird makes its roost in them during the long winter nights. And then, come the unending summer days, it skewers its beak into their sleep. So the light doesn't relieve, it only makes the blackbird thrive. After only a week of these white nights, I sympathise.

How quickly she is disappearing, just a faint shadow, waist deep. I take the rangefinder from my rucksack and point it at her. She is only five metres away. She has no ranging pole to steady her or warn of what's coming underfoot, no life jacket. A small freak wave, a stumble, is all it takes. The trickle starts and sucks you down into the topple that can't be fought. Going. Going. Boots of lead. A suit of lead. So very foolish.

Gone.

Just in case she doesn't return, and becomes a

celebrated mystery herself, a missing person, I take out my GPS. I stroke open the notebook and in the pages at the end I dedicate to such cases, I complete the prepared table with the date, time and grid reference.

Before leaving Edinburgh, I trimmed my nostril hairs and had a haircut in readiness for the photo I foresee, in *The Orcadian*. It will merit the whole front page—a high resolution studio shot of the solver of the mystery, with his mythical find. I'll be holding the creature by the neck, having caught it just before its drop into the sea, when it's still without feathers. There'll be a sniff of triumph in my expression. Who wouldn't feel it, with the prize money they're offering? But there'll also be a suggestion of sensitivity, a hand held towards the goose as if to say, 'Here it is, but how sad I couldn't bring it in alive'. And I'll tie a ribbon around its neck to show respect; a mark of the special occasion.

There are twenty-four hours to go.

A soft sucking noise comes from the sea ahead. And then more, louder, rhythmic. The gradual appearance of a form, like a photograph developing, emerging from the white. I score through my entry in the notebook. I could hardly have taken credit for her disappearance anyway.

As she approaches, her form sharpens. Grey-circled eyes. A blue clip in her hair. And something dangles now, from her hand. I grab at the binoculars. Did I miss it?

Suddenly, horribly, I see her face under *The Orcadian*

masthead. Tired but triumphant. Then the image is gone, like one of those subliminal frames in films that can unsettle you, that you're not even sure you saw. Anyway, she wouldn't hold it like that, by the neck—it would be under her arm, as if she was exhibiting prize poultry at a country show, or as if it's one of the cats that her type adopts in the wynds of Stromness.

But the image snags in my mind. Her as the finder of the tree-goose instead of me.

The day is edging towards midnight and there's still a burble of curlews, and oyster catchers squealing. A gull mourns high above me. It's like a kind of Chinese torture —the constant sound, perpetual light, nights without punctuation, just the evening descent of this small white room to wrap about one, to disorientate.

But we professionals know tiredness. It comes with the territory. We know danger too. Last year I abseiled alone into that well, not knowing how deep it was, and with a rucksack of timber on my back. There was just a coin of light above me, my fingers finding moss, a thick damp smell filling my head. But at the very darkest point, I found water that transforms wood into stone. And that earned me an entry in the other end of the notebook, for the mysteries I have solved rather than created.

'Hello, there!' I call out, standing up, raising my hand. I need to study her piece of driftwood.

The whites of her eyes flash against a face tanned from

these past hot days. But there's something sun-beddish about her, a bronze disguise to the washed-out look. Her hair is brassy even with the damp on it. She slides towards me.

'Didn't see you,' she says. 'I was in a dream.'

'Midsummer Night's?'

'Right.' She looks at her watch. 'It's after eleven. Can you believe this place?' She steps over the threshold and slumps onto a ledge in my look-out. Trusting, it seems. Or plain exhausted. She's dropped the driftwood behind her foot. I glimpse a cluster of encrusted shells. But I cannot tell from here if they're levering open, if they contain my treasure.

'My guest house,' she says. 'It's awful. There's no bleeding curtain. Haven't slept for nights. Going mad with it, I am.'

'Forced to walk abroad.'

'Just like being abroad, you're right,' she says. 'I didn't know you got heat like this so far north.'

'You're on holiday?' I ask.

Her hand flutters to the driftwood. By late June, according to John Gerard's *Third Booke of the Historie of Plants of 1597*, the shells should be ripe, parting to let the legs dangle out, a single stem attaching the bill to the shell's hinge, which will finally snap, dropping the body into the sea to spread its wings. With such a marine beginning it's no wonder that it raised the question during Lent, was the tree goose fish rather than flesh?

'It's a sort of holiday,' she says. 'And you?'

'Sort of.'

She narrows her eyes at me a little. I see moisture beaded on her upper lip. Sweating like me, in this still damp heat. I'm suddenly afraid she's going to leave with her trophy, before I've properly seen it.

'Busman's holiday for me,' she says. 'I'm a professional dowser, see. You know, finding water and that?'

'There's no shortage here, is there?'

She laughs. 'It's not just water we look for.'

'Oh?'

'You can use dowsing to solve anything. I've been all over—the Nazca desert drawings, even the Bermuda Triangle.'

'Not much of a living in that, I don't suppose,' I say. 'Solving mysteries.'

'You're wrong there. My dad built a dynasty on the family gift. Yacht in Turkey. House in Cyprus. There's rewards offered. People don't realise that.'

A cold grip in my gut. Her face on the front page of *The Orcadian* again, jewellery-encrusted. I hold her gaze. She holds mine. A white corridor between us, daring each other to sudden movements.

'So, you a twitcher, then?' She indicates the binoculars around my neck.

'In a way, my dear.'

'What's with all the gear? The big rucksack?'

'Sandwiches. Waterproofs.' I could go on with the list, but I don't.

There's a whistling sound behind us and the unmistakable smack of a golf swing.

'They're bonkers here. Did you hear that?' she asks.

I picture the flight of the white ball, lost until the morning sun beats back the haar. I mime ducking, hands protecting my head, and she laughs rather too loud and too long.

'Place driving *you* mad, and all?' she says.

She burbles like the birds, full of Croydon and travel plans, and her sore feet and aching limbs and the longing she has, the longing for the dark, and for sleep. Her tongue trips with it, unleashed to nonsense like she's spoken to no one for a week. It's as if I'm in a small room with her, the key being turned in the lock from the outside.

If there was night, proper night, she wouldn't be sitting here with me at twenty minutes to midnight, not with a complete stranger. She would go away, sleep. I would go away, sleep. Wake with cool reason. Wake without the sense that she's going to beat me to the mystery while my brain is unconscious.

She burbles and cackles and crows. Sweat collects around my hairline, leaching through too many clothes at my armpits. The key turning, turning. . .

Then it comes. A shooting star of creativity. Sheer mid-summer midnight brilliance.

'Listen,' I lean forward, level the excitement from my voice. 'I think I can help.'

'Help?'

Quietly, I say: 'With what you're looking for.'

She glances at the driftwood. But it's clear she's as unconvinced as I am that the closed shells contain tree geese.

'I see,' she says.

We are in that corridor again. But her dazed brain, missing its nightly release into unconsciousness, its return to order, makes her helpless.

I lead her across crisp, wind-toughened grass, turning to smile encouragement. Her waders squeak slightly, joining the chorus of birds. I know my way. I've had time to explore. I show my confidence as we walk through the sheet of daylight-night. Faint shadows of stones and dykes and mounds rise around us, lurk briefly and then vanish. It's as if she's in a trance, barely notices that we have climbed a little, left the shore. Drugged by the rhythm of the walking, by lack of reason, she follows.

It's only when I slide back the steel hatch of the chambered cairn, that she snaps into confusion.

'But I thought. They'll be in the sea, not . . .'

'Trust me.' I raise a hand of authority. 'It's the very thing you're after.'

166

The gentleman always, I gesture for her to climb down the ladder first, into the black. She makes a cooing sound as her head disappears. I've been in there already, know the relief of darkness, the eyes adjusting to see the texture of stone walls and graffiti close around you. I've seen the child-sized tunnels and chambers that lead from the main room. I've sat on the gravel floor and pondered what could happen here.

'It's so cool'. Her voice echoes up to me as I pause at the hatch, looking down.

'And dark?'

Her face is a pale oval, catching the light.

'Almost,' she says.

'Aha!'

This is where I can be most helpful. With one quick movement, I slide the steel hatch back into place, seal her into her longed-for darkness. Now she can sleep, halt the roaming and searching through the long white night. She is perfectly contained by a sepulchral gloom. She has the black-out she desires.

From my rucksack, I take the padlock and snap it through the hasp. Heavy and secure. When the Historic Scotland warden makes his fortnightly visit, he'll puzzle over it, but it might take another fortnight before he goes back with a hacksaw.

I take out the GPS, the notebook. In one end, I make a note of date, location, and time. Midnight exactly. Then I turn the notebook over to the end dedicated to 'solved' cases. I have all day tomorrow to make my entry there.

As I slide between cool white linen sheets, slip on my black blindfold for the sleep which will surely lighten my own darkness now, I thrill with the new mystery to be splashed across *The Orcadian* after I have left for the mainland: VISITOR MISSING.

The Searching Glance

THEN I WAKE up and hear that music on the radio. It's stealthy at first. Hushed footfalls approaching. They grow louder, as if a multitude is assembling, rustling against each other, surrounding the house. They bat soft wings against my bedroom window as if they want to get in. Or want me to go out.

There's a change in key, and a single voice bursts in on me with a thrill that stings in my toes and sits me up.

'Gorecki *Symphony Number Three*,' the presenter says when the music finishes.

I am summoned away from my barren bed. I get up and strip the sheets, shove them in the washing machine. I should have done it before—they're so heavy with night sweats and sadness.

I arrive breathless at the Art College reception, where a late-November day stares through the window. I stand under a bright lamp that warms the crown of my head.

The memory of the music still soars up from my feet into my stomach and chest. It rises in movements—slowing, pausing, rising again. I resist its pushes and pulls, try to stand still for the receptionist I have been brought before. She has a pen hanging from her mouth, and spectacles levered on top of her head. Her fingers riffle through papers and files.

Perhaps I smile accidentally, or fidget, because she looks at me for a blink, as if to catch me not paying attention. It only squeezes the feeling higher—to the top of my greying head where the host are a-flutter. If I open my mouth, I'm sure a white feather will float out to shock her, and make me laugh out loud.

'The start of the session was ages ago,' she says.

I hang my head, but only very slightly. I want to tell her that I had no idea I was supposed to come.

'There's this one. Starts tomorrow. Three weeks up to Christmas. Photography.' She lays a bright yellow flyer on the desk and I lift it against the darkening square of day at the window.

'That's the one,' I hear my voice say. 'I'll do it.'

And then she's having me sign things and write a cheque and telling me to be here prompt at nine thirty. Maybe my face is still creased by coils of bedclothes, because she looks at me doubtfully, as if I won't make it that early. But my promise hangs between us.

I make my purchase at HMV and then rush home to

play the music again. I stare into the mirror, waiting for the brighter face to rise behind the granite. I wait for the scratch of fingernails behind a hairline crack—a finger wriggling through until there's room for both hands to squeeze into the gap and push away from each other the two creaking boulders.

I smear honey in great dollops onto sliced bread— folding it into a sandwich. I know about honey—it's rich with calories, packed with life force. It stores the sun. In years past, I took it with ginger at this time of year for circulation, to fortify myself against the dark. I made cakes with it too—oatmeal and honey and hazelnuts, cut into crescents, baked brown and eaten under the stars. And once upon a time, I might have eaten honey for fecundity.

'Go out with a hungry eye,' the tutor says. 'See what it is your eye wants to eat, mmm?'

Each of us has a camera in our hands, a traditional 35mm so that we can get the hang of aperture settings and depth of field, and dark-room processes before we move on to digital work next week.

'"The searching glance",' he says. 'This is your brief. Your theme.' He looks around at our faces. 'Any questions, *muchachos*, before I send you out into the world?'

We look at our cameras. It's Adult Education, and we're not all young. Perhaps we're cowed by memories of our student days. I look at his sleek, white cropped head and tanned Spanish skin.

'What do you mean?' I ask. 'By "a searching glance"?'

He laughs and slaps his thigh. 'Thank you, thank you. I wait to see if anyone asks more. Brave lady. *Vamos a ver.* Let us see. What do I mean, mmm?'

The ones who already know each other scuff gazes, ask each other with the purse of a lip or a raised eyebrow.

'What's the nature of a glance, mmm?'

'It's brief,' offers one man.

'Shows only a bit of interest, not very much interest.' Someone else.

'But maybe it sparks off more. If the glance is reciprocated,' I offer.

'Aha.' He gleams. 'And what about "searching"?'

I follow in the wake of something, a flurry of air and excitement, towards the city centre to start my search. On the bus, I'm a head taller than the youngsters who are stacked up under my arms, mouths pushed against each others' chests, rucksacks bashing. We sway collectively with the movement of the bus, holding each other up. I raise the viewfinder to my eye once or twice but my finger won't depress the button. It feels a bit like theft to take pictures of people without their collaboration.

I retreat from the cold streets into cafés. There's one that's full of students. I feel invisible amongst them. I'm the only silent thing in a jungle of laughter, steam hissing, trays bashing into piles, and the occasional audible phrase of a song straining through the thick plasma of the café afternoon. I thaw and warm into the drowse of observation, fan myself discreetly with the menu when the flush rises in my face and neck. I watch life flickering by while my personal soundtrack rolls.

The students, with their cherub faces, seem incongruous in near-adult bodies. Boys' bums don't fill their jeans. They're in their first burst of independence—out drinking every night, eyeing the girls who seem so much more confident. There's a Japanese-looking boy with hands that flutter like mating birds, rising and falling above his lap. Perhaps he'll be a musician.

It's mostly girls I'm drawn to, though. I don't know why. I watch them in their groups. Out of the corner of my eye I see how laughter rocks the circle like a Mexican wave, catching at one point, and following around, like fire burning a dried wreath, starting and finishing at the same point.

I wait for that quality I want. It's called 'getting your eye in'. But already I can feel my material beckoning.

The girl has a nice smile, and looks me dead in the eye when it's my turn in the queue, but I don't dare ask her, even though I feel a playful rapport when I go back for the third time.

'Cappuccino. Very dry, please. Again.'

'Sure,' she says.

'Carrot cake looks good.'

'It's yummy. Like some?'

'I'd better I think. Low blood sugar's dangerous.'

The girl's hair is drawn up into a red scarf—hygiene regulations no doubt. It spurts from the bottom in a surprise of long tiny plaits, each one finished with a coloured bead. They bounce and spangle off her bare shoulders and arms. She wears one of those aprons that fits snugly about the hips, and wide jeans that flap around her feet. I suppose when I worked in cafés and bars at her age, middle-aged women looked at me in the same way, admiring the raw spirit of youth. But I only ever used to notice the men.

She comes to clear the table next to me.

'Yummy,' I point at the empty plate. 'Just like you said.'

'I eat it all day. My mum says it's not a balanced diet.' She laughs. 'But, hey. Life's short.'

The cake crumbles in my throat and angels' voices fade. Was it the mention of her mum? When I look up again, she's moved on, smiling at the group of uniformed schoolgirls at the next table.

At the sink in the café toilets, the mirror briefly frames the girl as she passes behind me. I put my hand in my bag, and it comes out smeared with white cream.

'Bastard thing', I mutter, and pull out the offending tube of moisturiser. ADVANCED HEALING the label says, and I wonder if a cream can really do that. Or indeed, if a photography project can. Grabbing at some paper towels, I mop up. I feel like crying and throwing the greasy contents of my bag across the room. But I also want to say, 'It's OK. Look. Clean now. There. What's the fuss for?'

I find my comb and lipstick, take my time. I hear the toilet flush and then our faces are side by side in the mirror as if they're both asking a question of it. There's something I'm trying to grasp about this picture, a tingle rising.

She leans forward, fingering her chin. 'Zits. Don't you hate that? It's working in all the steam.'

'I used to get them too. Just the same place. Feels like they're pulling your whole face towards them, doesn't it?'

The girl rubs gloss onto her lips. They are full, pouty, a bee-stung look that I might have had once. What is it, about those two faces side by side? Something.

'I wonder,' I turn to the girl rather than her reflection. 'Would you mind? I'm doing a photography project. Would you mind if I took your photograph?'

'Me?' Her hand rises over the zit on her chin.

'I'm a student,' I say. 'A mature student.'

She giggles. 'In here?'

'Outside's probably best.'

On the pavement, the grey afternoon will soon turn to

night. Passing tour buses are dampened from bright red to rust. Maybe a studio would be better. There's so little light. The girl's neck bends over her folded arms. She is cold, or embarrassed, or perhaps senses the torrent of questions dammed up in me—what's your name, and have you always lived in Edinburgh, and what age are you?

It's only the last one that I ask, and her reply hangs in my mind. Like the receptionist's fingers, I have a sense of riffling through suspension files, trying to find an answer.

'Let's just play a bit. Prance about. I'll snap,' I say.

She turns to me, looking to understand, and at that moment, I snap. I get her gaze I think, with a question in it. We both laugh.

'Is it colour, or black and white?'

'Colour. Your head scarf looks great.'

She pulls it off her head. It's bigger than it looked. She winds it around her neck, across her mouth and chin, her eyes laughing at the camera. Snap. She ties her plaits in it, pulls them straight above her head. Snap. She straps it across her tits, ties it loosely at the back. Snap. The laughter's jolting the camera now. She's quite a performer.

'Here.' She grabs the camera out of my hands. 'Let me take one of you.'

On the darkening pavement, lit by car headlights, jostled by people leaving work early for Christmas shopping and warm bars, she hands me the red scarf. I make a sling and hang my left arm in it. If I was working in the fields, a baby might be slung there in the same way, close to my heart. I shrug and she captures it, with a flash.

She looks back over her shoulder, into the café. There's a growing queue.

'Shit, Jean'll kill me.'

Then she's got the door open, is leaving me. I thrust the scarf into her hands.

'I'll come back. When I've got the prints,' I call after her.

Through the window I see that she takes up her position behind the counter again, and she's smiling. But she doesn't look out onto the dark pavement. Not at me.

Nineteen years old. Damn it. My mind has been working behind my back.

As I walk away into the city streets, I put the camera away in my bag, redundant now. It's suddenly night. Clear, with stars. This time of year is black and light—extremes that excite. Night extends and expands and life itself seems compressed into a small bright jewel. Lasers light avenues up into the sky. Music jangles in the cold air, and shrieks rise from the ice rink. A piper on the corner. Traffic. A Ferris wheel turns, its neon rim flashing in arcs off street windows. A slice of moon appears in the sky. As above, so below.

I think of the crescent shape of moon cakes. Honey, oatmeal, hazelnuts. And how before we ate them, we gathered naked in a woodland clearing, to wash each other with water from a huge pot. We twined evergreen leaves in each others' hair, lit candles, a fire. The chill of the water, the candle's shimmering reflection, the shiver of my own body, all watched by the men hiding in the trees. When they joined us, we drank wine, ate moon cakes, and knew that the sun would come back—that we'd helped the circle of the year to turn.

Near the Ferris wheel, a small boy is strapped into the bungey bounce. They set him off gently, his legs running in mid-air, scuffling faster as he nears the Earth.

'I thought he'd greet.' His mother sits on the wall next to me, talking to her own mother. Her eyes are glossy as her hand goes over her mouth.

The three of us watch as he swings up and over, a steep circular dance. His grin grows wider. The boy's hair is blond and curly, rising and falling against the air. I think how the mother will never know him when he's grey. All she can do is see him into the world, and then let him go. He bounces up to the apex, and swings back towards the Earth in that long, slow, inevitable arc.

A circle of fire draws me to Holyrood Park. As I get closer, within the range of low voices, the circle fragments, and I see that it's made by burning batons tossed between two figures. Red glows smatter off their hands and faces rhythmically, with the pattern of their exchange.

'Welcome,' a voice cries out, and I raise my hand, supposing it to be for me. I linger on the edge of the light. Dark figures squat in groups, silhouetted bottles raised to mouths, smoke rising from fingers, then passed sideways. Drums, low and rumbling. Gypsies I think, but doubt.

A nudge on my arm, and a bottle, that I swig from as if it's beer or wine. Whisky burns down to my toes. I see no faces.

A cry goes up—'Dance!' It's repeated in a chant, and then a figure bursts into a clearing in the crowd. Flesh glistens in the cold night. There's jangling and breath and drums. A mane and beads. Sinuous arms twist a red scarf above her head. She is illuminated by the laser rods in the crowd. I can feel her smile, because surely I can't see it. I can feel the feet, bare maybe, rising and falling. The crowd clapping, sweat glimmering her body. A car passing on the road flashes its headlights, and I see her face. Her eyes are right on me. A slight nod of her head.

The roar in me and the whisky, and the cord of connection, pulls me forward. I stamp my feet opposite her, gaze up to the stars, move in a small circle between her and the crowd, as she turns on her own axis in the centre. I encircle, protect, jump a star at each quarter, facing out into the shadowy mass of clapping spectators. At each jump, a deep cry hurls out of me into the night.

179

'It's the dry cappuccino lady,' she says at the end of the dance, wiping her forehead with the red scarf. She's holding a candle at chest height, so that her eyes are deep sockets.

A faceless figure passes, squeezing the girl's shoulder, asking, 'That your mum?'

'How did you know?' she asks. 'To come? We never advertise. It's just word of mouth.'

'I didn't know. Drawn by the firelight, I guess.'

'Coincidence,' she says, and looks at me a little too long.

'I wasn't. . .' I didn't follow you or anything, I want to say. I want to tell her how this whole day has been given to follow the tug of something that I cannot name.

'Good to see you, anyway.' She smiles. 'I'm going to get a drink.'

I allow myself to melt back into the darkness, shaken and unsure about why I came here.

When I return to the café a few days later with the prints, we sit down together. We drink cappuccino, and I buy us both a slice of honey cake.

'The zit didn't show too much after all,' she says.

I laugh.

'Do you have children?'

I stumble slightly on the cake, cough out my response. I've been asked directly like this in India. It's usually followed up with: 'Why not?'

My hands arrange photos on the table. I lay side by side the photo of her with her hair pulled upright, and the photo of myself.

'What do you think?' I ask.

'Cool.'

'I used to look something like you. More like you.' A sense of closing in. Getting warm.

She giggles. She doesn't see it.

'I was pregnant once.' It's out. 'But I didn't have it.'

'Miscarriage?'

Words are wedged somewhere deep. It would be easy to earn some sympathy here. 'No.'

She nods as she sips her coffee. 'A long time ago?'

'Nineteen years.'

I hear a soft click—perhaps just her breath. Then she looks up, a little alarmed, as if I'm going to claim to be her mother. She sees my eyes, and hands me the red serviette that came with the honey cake. I long to recover the promise of that day I first heard the music. Am I on a path back to the coiled bedclothes?

'Pity you're not a Buddhist.'

I look up.

'In Japan they believe that the soul of an 'unseeing' baby can be reborn. Later.'

'At my age?' I huff at her.

'It wouldn't be your baby—someone else's.' She holds my gaze. 'You don't deny them life. It's temporary.'

181

'How do you know all this?' I hold back the indignation. 'You're too young.'

'I'm studying anthropology.'

I nod.

'Have you ever thought of a ritual?' she asks.

'For what?'

'Your unborn child.'

'I used to do rituals, when I was younger. At the turn of the seasons. I think I might have out-grown them.'

She's looking at me.

'I guess I used to be more spiritual,' I say.

Her gaze makes me look at the table.

'What would it include, to be right for you?' She reaches out and takes my hand.

She brings sheets of red paper and shows me how to fold one, origami-style, to make a paper boat.

'I haven't done this since I was a kid,' I say.

The boat has a broad flat base, and inside it I stand a candle. She does the same with hers.

The river is dark below us. We hear it lapping up to us as we scramble down the frosty bank. Two women, similar in height and build, giggling as we slither, shivering slightly.

'Is there anything you want to say?' she asks when we stand on the edge, our feet almost in the water.

I look straight at the blank dark space where I know her

face is. I want my unseeing child to have been reborn in this beautiful, wise young woman. I reach out and touch her chin, gently. I taste the sweetness of the words that wheel inside me, drawing saliva to them, but they refuse to cut through the night air. 'Please forgive me,' remains a thought.

Instead, words arrive from long ago, and spill from me: 'I shall know always there is light. I shall know always there is hope of life to come.'

When I light the candle I see that her face is shining.

We kneel on the river bank and launch our twin boats. Her hair jangles softly, and the voices start to soar through my head again. I sense a hushed gathering behind us, the rime-winged presence who ushered me here.

The girl and I stand up and watch two small jewels of fire gleam away from us, sailing downstream.

Acknowledgements

Thanks to Michael B Harrison and the writers who met over lunch at Terregles Avenue for giving invaluable feedback on these stories, and to my agent, Jenny Brown, for her unstinting support. I also acknowledge the support from the Scottish Arts Council towards the writing of this collection.

With thanks to Charlotte Brontë's 'The Professor' for the character of Yorke Hunsden in 'Le Grand Jeté', and to Fairway Forklifts for inspiring 'Angel Face'.

Acknowledgments and thanks are due to the editors and BBC producers who gave stories their first airing as follows:

'The Smell of Growth': BBC Radio 4, The afternoon reading, September 2003 and *Stepping into the Avalanche*, Brownsbank Press, 2003; 'Over the Garden Wall', *Edinburgh Review*, 2006; 'A Sense of Belonging', *Mslexia*, April 2005; 'Angel Face', *Southlight*, 2006; 'Beneath the Coat Pile', *Word Jig, New Fiction from Scotland*, Hanging Loose Press, New York, 2003 and *Stepping into the Avalanche*, Brownsbank Press, 2003; 'And the Sky was Full of Crows', *Northwords Now*, Spring 2006; 'The Match', *The Hope That Kills Us, An anthology of Scottish Football Fiction*, Freight Design/Polygon, 2002; 'Kiss of Life', *Damage Land, New Scottish Gothic Fiction*, Polygon, 2001 and *Lie of the Land*, Perth & Kinross, 2004; 'The Weight of the Earth and the Lightness of the Human Heart', *North*, Polygon, 2004; 'Le Grand Jeté', BBC Radio 4, The afternoon reading, May 2005; 'Night's High Noon', BBC Radio 4, The afternoon reading, Nov 2006.

Lightning Source UK Ltd.
Milton Keynes UK
UKHW03f0957290418
321814UK00001B/152/P